AFTER THE GREAT
DEVASTATION

AFTER THE GREAT DEVASTATION

BY
DANA PRIDE

Everlasting Publishing
Yakima, Washington
USA

After the Great Devastation

by
Dana Pride

Library of Congress Control Number
2010940587

ISBN: 0-9824844-9-6

ISBN-13: 978-0-9824844-9-4

First Edition
Everlasting Publishing
P.O. Box 1061
Yakima, WA 98907

This book was inspired by a dream God gave me.
Be true to the dream.

For my dad,
Joseph Fram

and in honor of my great-grandparents,
Obiad and Sun Maloof

AFTER THE GREAT DEVASTATION

CHAPTER 1

I was at work. It seemed like I was always at work, and I didn't really mind it. I had been going there since I was eight years old, although at that early time it was hard to tell the training part, which to me was like playing games, from the work part, which was also like playing games. That was the way they got the young people involved at a young age, when they discovered someone had a specific talent or knack. As soon as the gift was identified, the kid would be swooped up and trained or channeled into the area to hone that gift, to become the best he or she could be. I didn't like the label they put on us, 'Kidgen' for a kid genius, but it was better than some of the alternatives: 'Ordin' for the Ordinaries; 'Crim' for the Criminals, even if they had only been caught one time breaking the law; the 'Runners,' who ran all over the place, doing errands for everyone else; and then there were the 'Chairs,' the huge people who lived in chairs and had Runners get for them what they needed. I worked with other Kidgens and the Comgens, the computer geniuses. I had a really fun job, although I didn't like to think of it as a career, something I would be doing all my life, since in that job I was so isolated at my workstation, and I liked to spend a lot of time with other people and outside.

Oh, they tried to accommodate us. It seemed like everything we asked for or even mentioned that we desired, they would provide. Like when they first brought me to the Complex, I mentioned that I liked ice skating. Well, inside the Complex it was so crowded, or should I say, every space was being efficiently used, so, I said to some of my co-workers, it would be nice to be able to skate all the way around the Complex, on the outside. I don't know who made the decisions around there, and, at that time, I didn't even know anyone was listening to my conversation; but soon a canal was built and filled with water, all the way around the Complex, and in the winter it was frozen so we could skate on it. It was at least several miles around the perimeter, and it was really a fun skate, wide enough for several people to skate holding hands. Also it was very smooth for skating and it was flat enough, with just a little incline. We skated up one side and down the other, as we went around the giant loop. When spring came and the ice was starting to melt, they decided to make the canal into a swimming channel, and that was fun, too, in the summer when it was so hot outside. Then in the summer, when I mentioned I liked roller skating, they built a nice, smooth path around the canal. Some people rode their bikes on it, others walked on it, so, it was a good use of the resource, since not everyone loved to skate as much as I did.

It was a weird kind of freedom that we had, we Insiders who lived in the Complex. We would go to work when we wanted and take breaks when we wanted, as long as we finished our tasks on time. My job was really fun, like playing a game. They discovered when I was young that I had a gift for decoding and seeing patterns in codes, so they snatched me up and started giving me all these games to play. Later, I knew they were training me, but when I first started, I thought I was just playing games and working puzzles. And that was what I was still doing, nine years later, playing games, decoding codes, and working puzzles at the Complex.

They didn't know I had started doing these kinds of things much earlier, when my dad used puzzles for testing people when I was just two and three years old. He would bring the puzzles home to figure out how they worked, and I would dive in and solve the puzzles before he could even read the instructions. They thought I didn't have any early memories of my Life Before, but even at age eight, I knew enough to keep them to myself. After all, my memories were all I had of my Life Before. I had only fragments of memories, mostly of my dad and me, and many of my mom, who was so beautiful with her blond hair and green eyes, and her soft voice and her kindness. My young mind must have blocked out the Day of Devastation. I couldn't remember anything about it at all, even after reading about it and seeing the video.

Big Hawk said I didn't remember because it didn't really happen the way they said it happened, so we were only getting carefully controlled propaganda, video and 'news,' and he was probably right. He was a different kind of Kidgen; so very smart, but he was also defiant. I mean, they would never would have guessed, but in private, he was always telling us, his friends, the truth about what really happened in every situation, since he had access to all kinds of information, as well as a photographic memory. The rest of us were pretty compliant. That's not to say we didn't have our pranks and secrets, but we followed the rules and we did what was expected of us to do to help the general order of things.

So, I was at work when Kenrick sent me a PM, a private message. When others sent a PM, I was pretty sure they weren't really private, but since Kenrick was a Comgen, he had ways to send messages that couldn't be traced, tracked, intercepted or in any way read by anyone else, and as soon as I read his message, it dissolved into a cool graphic, so, even if someone figured out that I received a transmission from him, it could only be recalled as a graphic. I think it had something to do with layers, and the top layer could never be recalled. Anyway, Kenrick sent me a message, an invitation to go to his pod with Big Hawk and Hiding Cathy. I had never been to his pod before, but he said he had ordered some kind of great foreign meal and he wanted to share it with us.

Oh, that was another cool thing about the Complex, besides the fact that everything we needed was inside it, from food to entertainment to clothes to our work, we lived there, so, we didn't have to commute. I had heard about the horrors of commuting in Life Before, especially since the global gas shortage when all the old vehicles had been abandoned all over the place and were, in many areas, blocking the roads. That meant the mini solar cars could only travel in certain areas. Everyone who worked at the Complex lived at the Complex. They said we were free to travel, with proper authorization, but kids never traveled without adults. I hadn't traveled since I came to live at the Complex. I didn't miss traveling. Where was there to go?

I had seen on the monitors how horrible life was Outside the Complex, with all the pollution and the Runners and the Crims and the dangerous food. A few times I watched the transmissions that were being sent to the Outsiders, our nickname for everyone who didn't live in the Complex, and it was loaded with implications that soda pop and compact foods and chemical mixtures were real food. Their only choice of things to eat was from a selection of stuff that wasn't really food. Their menu was made up of a myriad of substances, pressed and shaped to resemble real food and drinks. Whereas we Insiders consumed only whole natural organic food and drink which was properly prepared for us fresh daily, the Outsiders drank mixtures of water with artificial colors and flavors and they ate processed dried food, mostly covered with chocolate and flavored with sugar. It was obvious to us why they were always so sick and weak and they had so many mental problems – their food contained no nutrition. The Admin of the Complex said that was nature's way of keeping us healthy while letting them survive a shorter time, to not let them suffer very long from all the diseases that were out there. As one of our cooks once told me, "You are what you eat. We are whole, natural and organic. The Outsiders eat nothing but junk, so, what does that say about them?" I felt sorry for the Outsiders, since they didn't have access to real food, but the attitude of the Insiders was that the Outsiders didn't know what they were missing – and besides, they liked it! They liked to eat fake food! I almost couldn't believe it, but then, I knew they were different from us. Their whole lives were different, their lifestyles were different, their attitudes about life were different.

At precisely the same moment, Kenrick, Big Hawk, Hiding Cathy and I left our workstations, went and washed our hands, and walked through the Complex to Kenrick's pod. The guys lived on the south side of the Complex, the girls on the north, and the married couples were interspersed among both sides.

"You won't believe what I was able to get!" Kenrick told us as we were walking. He always spoke very quickly, so we really had to pay attention to what he was saying in order to understand him.

"Goat cheese?" Big Hawk asked enthusiastically. He always asked for goat cheese, and that was one item that was close to impossible to get at the Complex. I knew we had lots of cows and sheep and chickens that were grown somewhere Outside, but we had no goats.

"No, I–" Kenrick began.

"Watermelon?" Hiding Cathy asked. She loved watermelon, but we could only get it at a specific time of year. For some reason, it didn't grow well in our greenhouses, and we couldn't get it from anywhere else anymore.

"No, wrong again. It is not watermelon. Any more guesses?" Kenrick asked.

"No idea," I said, shaking my head. I couldn't imagine what exotic food item he had found for us.

"Unless it could possibly be Moo Goo Gai Pan," Big Hawk said. Big Hawk was called Big Hawk because he was nearly seven feet tall, always looking down on the rest of us like a hawk, and the name distinguished him from Little Hawk, the security guard who had a nose like a hawk and was just under 5 feet tall.

"We can get Moo Goo Gai Pan any time we want it,

or at least once a week, if we ask for it," I reminded him. I wondered if Big Hawk was implying anything, since Kenrick's ancestors were of Asian descent. Big Hawk was often implying something and I didn't always want to figure out what he meant with his double-sided remarks.

"Yeah, but I missed it last week. I worked straight through and it was gone by the time I got to the Eatery," Big Hawk said, "and you know how much I love it."

"Well, it's not Moo Goo Gai Pan," Kenrick said.

"So, what is it?" Hiding Cathy asked.

"Have you ever had stuffed grape leaves?" Kenrick asked.

"How can you stuff a grape leaf?" Big Hawk asked. "It's flat." He held out the palm of his hand, to make his point.

"Oh, I know," I said. "It's not really stuffed, it's rolled. The stuffing is rolled into the grape leaves."

"Yeah!" Kenrick shouted, bobbing his head and getting excited. It was a pleasure to see him get excited, because he became so passionate about things, like a little kid. Sometimes I forgot that we were still little kids – well, maybe not so little, but still kids. Not very many younger people worked at the Complex, due to the sterilization after-effect of the bombings. Most of the people who had been born after The Great Devastation had to be institutionalized with full-time care. The genetics specialists were working to correct that, but that was one of the areas where man had done the damage and only God would be able to fix it.

"So, what's the stuffing?" Big Hawk asked, licking his lips.

"The ones I had before were made with rice and beef and chopped up tomatoes and onions and spices," Kenrick said.

"What kind of spices?" Big Hawk asked, as if he were going to make it and he needed the exact recipe.

"Um, I think garlic and something else," Kenrick said.

"Something else like what?" Hiding Cathy asked. We were approaching the steps to Kenrick's pod.

"Mint," I said. I somehow remembered stuffed grape leaves, from way back in my Life Before.

"Mint?" Kenrick asked. "Hmm, that could be it."

"Well, open the door! Let's eat!" Big Hawk said. We didn't usually eat in our pods, but we were allowed to have food and eat it there if we wanted. We could do pretty much what we wanted to do when we wanted to do it, as long as we didn't break the rules, and they had no rule against eating in our pods. I didn't like to bring too many foods to my pod because then I had to clean up the mess and take the dirty dishes back to be washed at the Eatery, and that was time spent that I didn't want to waste.

Kenrick opened the door to his pod and at first glance, I thought it was a two-person pod because of the layout, then I distinctly knew this double pod was all Kenrick's place. He had made it unique!

His pod had two segments, two rooms that were perpendicular to each other, each about 20 feet long and about 15 feet wide. We entered at the point where the two rooms joined. One segment went straight back and the other went off to our left. Each room had a washroom at the far end. The sides of the rooms were covered with bookshelves, and the bookshelves were filled with books and electronic equipment, and monitors were mounted all over the walls. On one side, at the end of one room, he had set up a little kitchen area with a counter and four chairs, a little refrigerator and a little oven. He walked over to it while we stood and stared at the room. He had no bed, no comfortable chairs, just one computer chair with wheels and a long table sitting in the middle of each room. Above each of the tables, hanging from the ceilings, were something like tents, or maybe they were tents, one in each room, and they were firmly attached to the ceilings. I looked at them curiously, wondering what they could be.

"You sleep up there?" Big Hawk asked, stretching one of his long legs to step up onto one of the tables. He had to bend his neck to prevent bumping his head on the ceiling. He unzipped the tent and stuck his head inside it.

"The only place to sleep," Kenrick said.

"This is so cool!" Big Hawk said, climbing up into the tent. He zipped it and there he was, inside a tent, suspended above the table. He was so big, I was surprised he fit inside it – but I wasn't surprised that the tent stayed attached to the ceiling beams. Kenrick was a stickler for details – he would have calculated the weights and the loads and the strengths to be sure the tent would not come tumbling down from the ceiling.

Hiding Cathy was hiding again. I almost didn't notice her under the table, all hunkered down in a little ball. Her white-blond hair looked like a tiny scarf that had been tossed onto a pile of clothes, which was her little body.

"I love sleeping up there, just hanging out," Kenrick

said. "It's the only way to sleep, suspended, like, sleeping in the clouds or something."

"Yeah, and you don't have any room for a bed on the floor, anyway," I added.

"This is true, so truer than true," Kenrick agreed, nodding. He took the food out of his refrigerator and put it a dish, then he put the dish in his little oven.

Immediately the smell of the cooking grape leaves took me back to my Life Before. A flash of a memory: so long ago, my mom made stuffed grape leaves because my dad loved them. I didn't really care for them at that time, but right now, they smelled like the best food in the world. They smelled like my childhood. It was amazing how a scent could take me back like that.

I looked around the room at all the computers and electronic equipment. They let Kenrick have any type of equipment he wanted, because the more he played, the more he learned. Some of his monitors were showing different locations in the Complex; others had games in progress. Some were disconnected, taken apart, open for us to see the insides of the computers.

He motioned for us to climb up onto the long table, so I did. He had to coerce Hiding Cathy out of her hiding place, and he helped her get on top of the table. We were standing with our faces just outside the tent where Big Hawk was.

"You can say anything here," Kenrick commented.

Big Hawk popped his head out of the tent, and his face was right with ours as we stood on the table.

"Say what?" he asked.

"Say anything you want to say, anything at all," Kenrick said. "This is a Water Closet-free zone."

"They have those?" Hiding Cathy asked. I didn't know of any place where our Watch-Communicators, or Wat-Coms, didn't work. The four of us had reduced the name to WC, then we picked up the old term 'Water Closet,' just to mess with anyone who might be listening and wouldn't know what we were talking about. Most people had no idea what a Water Closet was, which, to us, was just a convenient use of initials.

"They don't have them anywhere else, but I made one here," Kenrick said. "When I sleep here, they can't feed me any Prop," he said.

He was referring to the propaganda, which we all lived on, which was the source of our very survival, the subliminal messages constantly being pumped into our minds. As I looked more closely at the room, I noticed an almost invisible web of wires behind the bookshelves. I looked at my WC, and, sure enough, I didn't see the time or any pending communication. It didn't appear to be working, but I knew Kenrick was right – he had created a free zone in his room.

"They can't pick up anything we say here," Kenrick said.

"That is sooooo cooooool!" Big Hawk said. "So, what do we want to say that we don't want them to hear?"

I couldn't think of anything at that time. Hiding Cathy shrugged her shoulders.

"Really, we only have a couple of minutes," Kenrick explained, "since the odds that no one will check the status of any of us for any longer amount of time decrease with each minute."

What he said made sense, but it didn't really make sense. With our mandatory WCs we were required to always be available, but, as we all knew, in order to monitor all of us at all times, they would need a one-on-one observer for each of us, and in the Complex, they needed to utilize the skills and gifts of each person. They didn't have people who could waste all day every day observing someone else who lived at the Complex. However, with four of us out of detection, at any minute someone could want one of us and they could discover that they couldn't track any of us. They knew we were friends.

"So, why are we here?" Hiding Cathy whispered. "What's going on?"

"Yeah, what's the big secret?" I asked, my curiosity rising.

"You don't have to whisper, they can't hear us at all when we are up here," Kenrick said in his normal voice. "Anyway, I'm going to hook up some travel for us."

"Seriously?" I asked, amazed. I hadn't been beyond the Wall around the Complex since I came to live there. This could really be fun, travel with friends!

"More serious than you've ever been," Kenrick said.

"Kenny, how can you do that?" Hiding Cathy asked.

"I've already got it started," Kenrick said. "I've entered a travel agenda in each of our profiles, so we can get out of here for awhile. It has already been authorized, and no one will miss us."

"What are you talking about?" Big Hawk asked. "I haven't even traveled in so long, I don't know where we'd go. Where is there to go?"

"Where are we going?" I asked. I couldn't imagine where we might go on a secret journey.

"I will take care of everything, don't worry," Kenrick said. "This is going to be great."

"When are we going?" Big Hawk asked.

"You will see," Kenrick said mysteriously.

"Well, it's not like I have anything to do or anything, except work, I mean, nothing is coming up on my agenda that I would miss," Big Hawk added.

"Yeah, all we have to do is work," I said, "so, if you can get us out of work, I'm absolutely free. I would have all the free time in the world! Let's go! Whenever you get it set up, I mean."

"Don't worry about a thing," Kenrick said.

"Are we going to fly?" Hiding Cathy asked tentatively. She looked so scared, I thought she was going to hide again, maybe under the table or scrunched down on the bottom shelf of the bookcase. She was so small, so frail, so flexible, she could make herself tiny and still, and no one would even notice she was there. That was one reason she was so valuable to the State.

"Maybe," Kenrick teased. "Look, I'll let you know where and when."

"Don't we have to get our stuff ready or something?" I asked. I didn't really know what anyone needed to do to get ready to travel.

"Don't worry about anything. I'm going to take care of everything. I've got it all planned out, everything we will need, and I will give you the details later," Kenrick said, stepping off the table. "How about those stuffed grape leaves?"

Hiding Cathy and I sat on the edge of the table and scooted to the floor. Big Hawk came down out of the hanging tent and we all washed our hands. We sat in Kenrick's little kitchen and we ate the stuffed grape leaves. We enjoyed the stuffed grape leaves! We ate them with our fingers and we licked our fingers when the grape leaves were all gone. We decided to ask for this recipe to be put on as a regular menu option, at least once or twice a month. We knew better than to discuss our travel plans, once we were out of the WC-free zone. I had a million questions for Kenrick, and I was sure Hiding Cathy and Big Hawk did also, but we had to wait until later to ask them. When would we go? How would we escape from the Complex? Where would we go? What would we take? Who else would know about this? How would we cover ourselves while we were gone? How long could we dare to stay away? Would we be flying? Would we go outside the State? Would we be able to see any trees? (I still remembered trees.) Did we need currency or barter outside the Complex? Who would we visit?

We knew about Outsiders using currency and barter, but, as employees of the Complex, we didn't need to purchase anything. Everything we needed was provided for us. We didn't own any currency. All we had to do was to walk into any of the Complex shops and get whatever we wanted. Of course, our pods were not very big, so, we couldn't just load up on everything we saw – but who wanted to do that, anyway? We could go to the entertainment centers and enjoy all types of diversions at any time. We could change our wardrobes at any time. When we were younger and still growing, the clothes we outgrew would be given to some lucky Outsider, or, possibly, put in one of their barter shops. We worked for our food, we worked for our clothing and entertainment, and anything we desired was fantastically provided for us. It was a great feeling of satisfaction, just knowing that our work was taken seriously and an important service for the State, in exchange for everything we needed.

My friends and I were aware that some of the anti-propaganda on the Outside labeled us as evil and controlling and undermining, but they didn't take into consideration that the work we did protected everyone, Inside and Outside the Complex. We labored for the good of all. The ironic thing was that the Outsiders who were pushing the Anti-Prop campaign were the same ones who didn't work, who expected their handouts every week, without one bit of effort on their part. They didn't want to work. They didn't want to help anyone. They didn't want to join forces to keep our State strong and alert. They just wanted to be paid to be entertained at all times. I was so thankful that I had never been a part of that user mentality. We were doers, we were givers, we were helpers. We were Insiders.

I felt a buzz on my wrist, a reminder that I was one of the Insiders. Kenrick and Hiding Cathy looked at their Wat-Coms and I knew we were all getting the same message – some urgent matter had popped up and we had to return to our workstations as soon as we could. As I read my transmission, I wondered how long they had been listening to us. I wasn't worried that they had heard anything about our travel plans, and I knew our meal conversation had been more than dull to anyone who had been listening. They probably thought that just because we were Kidgens and Comgens, we had no excitement in our little lives. They just had no idea what we were capable of accomplishing.

CHAPTER 2

While sitting at my workstation, staring at the patterns and wondering how long to make them think I was working – I had decoded it so quickly, I was already finished, but I wanted to make them think I was really working hard, really concentrating – a huge excitement ball of fire was growing inside me. I felt like leaping, singing, shouting for joy… but I had to hold it inside, not let anyone know that we had a secret, we had a plan, we had a goal that didn't include them. I was hoping my pulse was not increased, or it would send a signal through my WC and I would need to go to the infirmary to be checked. That had happened to me one other time, when we were planning a surprise party for Kenrick, but at that time, I was able to convince the Health Official who examined me that I was just excited because I had cracked an incredibly difficult and important code pattern, which was true, but that wasn't why my heart rate had increased. It was increased because it was almost impossible to keep a secret from Kenrick, who had connections and communications everywhere, and we had done it for nearly two weeks. They thought the only thing we could ever get excited about had to do with work. I guess they figured that Kidgens were kind of like machines, without feelings or lives outside of our workstations. They didn't see the look of surprise on Kenrick's face when he walked into the entertainment auditorium, expecting to repair a faulty communicator, and we all came out of the woodwork, shouting his name. They didn't know we could have fun with people. We were not robots. We were kids with gifts.

I was suddenly tired and I wanted to go catch a nap. Using my Wat-Com, I signaled my supervisor that I had completed my task, he replied that he knew I could do it, and I walked across the Complex to my pod. The scents from the Eatery were floating around in the air, but I was still full of grape leaves, and more tired than anything. I opened the door to my pod and decided the décor was too dull. I liked bright colors and beautiful patterns. This pod said nothing about my personality, except that I had let some adult decorate it years ago and I had never changed it. I didn't spend much time there, but at that moment, I wanted it to be more like a home to me, the way Kenrick's pod reflected his personality. Oh, sure, I had a few books and a bright turquoise bedspread, but other than that, this could have been some old lady's (or old man's!) pod. I wanted to paint the walls bright colors and bring in some other embellishments, to make this pod look like my own pod. But not right now. Now all I needed to do was get some sleep.

I turned up the temperature of my bed – I could fall asleep very quickly when it was warm – and I washed my hands, put on my sleeper, and climbed under the covers. I slept in three-hour segments, usually three or six hours, once in a while nine, and then I usually went back to work for a shift until I got hungry again. Right at this time I didn't have any pressing business at work, so I opted for a nine hour nap. I loved them, because during the final segment I always had fantastic dreams – and sometimes, dreams of my family. I was hoping one would come tonight. I was so glad they hadn't perfected the Dream Recorder yet – my dreams were my own private source of pleasure that I didn't want to share with anyone, or, God forbid, have watched and analyzed by someone who wanted to try to figure out what was going on in my mind.

As I lay there, expecting sleep to overtake me

immediately since I was so tired, my mind reviewed the events of the afternoon. Kenrick was planning travel for us, all four of us! We were going to go somewhere outside the Complex, without real permission! I knew it would look like we had real permission. We could never get out of the Complex without our profiles stating that we had been cleared to leave; but we were going to go somewhere that WE wanted to go, not where they wanted us to go. I was trying to remember if Kenrick or Big Hawk had ever been allowed travel before, when we were younger, before we were friends – I knew they hadn't gone anywhere in the past few years. I knew Hiding Cathy had been outside the Complex many times. Her hiding skills were used to observe and investigate without detection, but she had been watched as closely by the State as the Outsiders she had been watching. She told me she had always been so afraid, she hadn't been able to enjoy her freedom. Actually, how could they call it freedom, when she was under tighter reins outside the Complex than any of us ever were inside? She had been able to see trees, though.

Would we see trees? I remembered them... they were tall, much taller than people, taller than buildings, taller than the Wall and even taller than the Complex! One tree could have all different colors – some were pink in the spring, green in the summer, orange and red and yellow in the autumn, and then the branches were bare when it was winter. Branches, a funny word, I hadn't thought about it in a long time, in that reference. We had Branches at work, and the Gen Branch rarely associated with the other Branches. We were not covered with colorful, changing leaves that fell off every year... how could we be called Branches? Another memory flash: in my Life Before, my mom and dad had taken me to a place crowded with trees, a type of place that didn't exist any more, where the trees were so thick, a person could hide in them or get lost in them, so even aerial surveillance couldn't see the person. At that time, there had been more trees than people. Imagine that... now we couldn't even find a tree, although reports were that some groups of trees still existed, somewhere. Maybe we would see some of them when we escaped and took our travel.

I startled myself when I considered that we would be escaping. We were not running away or trying to undermine anyone or the system, we were just going to travel on our own, for a short time (I guessed it was a short time) and then we would come back. When we returned, everything would be once again as normal, and most of our co-workers wouldn't even know we had been gone. We really weren't planning to do anything wrong. We were just going to have a little fun, a little bit of unauthorized fun, and when it was over, our lives would continue at the Complex, the same as they always had. I drifted into sleep visualizing trees.

My dreams during my third sleep segment reminded me that my life had not always been like this. It was not the same as it always had been. I was back, as a child, with my mom and my Aunt Moon, and we were enjoying one of our many carefree days. My dad and my Uncle Pierce were still alive, and we had plenty of time to take pleasure in living. I watched my mom and her sister, who looked so alike with their curly blond hair and green eyes, as they talked to each other in sister-speak and laughed and laughed together. I didn't really hear what they were saying to each other – it didn't matter, they weren't talking to me anyway – but we were just sharing our time together while we were in a foreign land, living a strange life, but a fun life.

As I returned to my own body and the realization that I was no longer little and no longer with my family hit me like a crate of computers, I felt sad. Where had my childhood gone? Why had it been stolen away from me? I missed my mom.

They tried to take away my memories of my family. I had to pretend I didn't remember, but I could remember snippets from my Life Before and After The Great Devastation, although I had no memory of the actual event; just the changes it made. We were living a free life, outside; then I was living a controlled life, inside. I was living with my family; then I was living away from my family. My mom was happy, loving, joyful, energetic; then she was silent, lifeless, staring. My Aunt Moon was with us; then she was gone. My dad and my Uncle Pierce were alive; then they were dead. I just was a regular kid; then I was a Kidgen.

My dad often used to tell me I wasn't a regular kid. He told me I was special and gifted, but wasn't that what all dads told their daughters? He called me 'La-la' because when I was a baby, I couldn't say 'Layla.' I called myself 'La-la,' and he thought it was a cute name. He kept it as his special name for me. I knew my dad wasn't a regular dad. He was special. He was so very kind and so very smart, although he had a look and a presence about him that made people afraid of him when they first saw him. Then his face would transform when he smiled, and they would be assured that he was their friend, on their side, and nobody better mess with them because he would protect them. His dark brown hair and dark brown eyes that he had passed down to me gave him a distinguished look, along with his broad shoulders and that air of confidence he always had. When I looked into his eyes I saw a kindness that was impossible to describe. My dad was the best dad there was; my parents were the best parents any kid ever had.

Since I had been at the Complex, I had been told repeatedly how lucky I had been to have had so many years with such wonderful parents. Apparently, Before The Great Devastation most kids had absent parents or addict parents, and After The Great Devastation there had been so few babies born, they had to be taken from their parents to the institutional growing stations to be nurtured, to try to make sure they would survive long enough to become kids. But I didn't feel lucky. I did have wonderful parents, then I lost them! I wasn't complaining about my life; I had everything I needed, but I missed the love they gave me, freely, every day. No matter what they gave us at the Complex, nothing could replace love.

At that time, I believed my mom was still alive, although I had not been able to visit her in years. The last time I saw her, she was in a Home, where they put what they unofficially called the Useless Outsiders. Wow, they would never let an Outsider hear that term, but I heard it sometimes, and it hurt me to think that was how they classified my mom. However, when I had visited her, she was there but she wasn't there. Her body was there, in the bed, but her mind was not with her. Her green eyes had become dull: they had lost their sparkle; they had lost their life. She didn't recognize me – she didn't recognize that I was even there. Big Hawk told me they kept all the Useless heavily drugged, so they couldn't fight or argue or cause any problems. When I was young, I was just so glad she was still alive, and I still had hope that she would get better and we would be reunited. Then, as I got older and I realized they were doing this to her, I got angry – so very angry, yet

I had to control my anger. (We Insiders were notorious for controlling our anger; we didn't want to be given any submission substances.) At one point, I thought it would be easier for everyone if they just killed the Useless, instead of drugging them, but I heard rumors they were trying to keep some women alive, the ones who had had children Before The Great Devastation, just to see if they could implant a child. I hadn't heard of any success in that area, but I knew it was a very quiet subject. The only information we could get were the coded messages Kenrick intercepted and I decoded. The messages on that topic were very few in number, so we knew it hadn't happened yet.

Anyway, I had visited my mom's outer shell a few times and I had cried, hoping my tears or the sound of my pleading would snap her out of her unresponsive state. I didn't understand how she could go from being the most loving mom in the world to a mom who didn't even know her daughter within such a tiny time span. Possibly they would have let me visit her again, but it hurt me too much to see her like that, without one bit of change or improvement in her condition. They certainly didn't encourage me to visit her again.

One thing I thought was very odd: they never let me see my Aunt Moon. I didn't know what happened to her. I had asked about her many times, and each time I was told that they would let me know later, but they never did. They wouldn't answer my questions, so I had no idea where she had gone. Had she become an Outsider? Was she in a Home like my mom? If she had died at some later date, would they have told me? It was as if they hoped I would just forget I ever had a family so I could do the best job possible for the State. Of course, I did my best, but my work wouldn't have suffered if they had allowed me to be with my family, or even hear news about them.

I heard a light tap on the door of my pod, and even without checking the scanner, I knew it was Hiding Cathy coming to see me. I pushed off my covers and opened the door for her. She immediately went into the bathroom and washed her hands, then she sat beside me on the bed, swinging her legs. I didn't know how old she was. I thought she was about my age, but if she wanted to pass for 8 years old, she could do it successfully – yet she was so smart, so wise, she could have been 50 years old.

"Sleeping?" she asked, looking at my sleeper.

"I was," I answered. "Just woke up."

She began to speak to me in sign language, something all the Kidgens knew and very few of the adults could understand. We were out of the view of any of the cameras, so we knew we could be heard through our WCs but not seen. Our silent conversation was out of their range.

"I am really looking forward to our travel," she signed.

"Me, too!" I responded, also in sign. "Any idea where we will go?"

"No idea," she answered. "It's up to Kenny."

Hiding Cathy, because of the very nature of her talent, was allowed to go on the Outside. As a matter of fact, she was encouraged to go, and they used her as a spy, to find out what the Anti-Prop group was planning. She had visited lots of places, and she had seen Outsiders first hand.

"We'll have to leave our Water Closets, you know, so

they can't track us," she signed.

"Oh, yeah, I didn't think of that," I responded. "But won't they know, I mean, how can we?" I asked. "The sensors will inform them as soon as we remove them."

"What they taught me to do is to leave mine on a cow's leg," she signed, giggling.

"You know a cow?" I almost asked that out loud, but instead I just laughed as I signed it. Hiding Cathy knew a cow!

"They can't really track our temperature once we get Outside, but they can tell if the WC gets cold, like if we just leave it on the ground or in a box or something."

"So, you go to your friendly cow and leave your WC, then just go back and get it when you're done with your mission?"

She nodded, laughing.

"How do you find the same cow?" I had a picture in my mind of Life Before, when herds of cows would be grazing in a field. I hadn't thought about where cows were kept these days.

"There are some cows not far from the Complex," she explained. "Where do you think we get our milk?"

"I didn't know it was so close, I mean, real cows, so close to the Complex?"

"Yes," she signed. "You know, we'll have to wear a scar."

I hadn't thought about that either! Every Outsider had a scar on his forehead where his implant had been inserted, to distinguish the Outsiders from the Insiders. Like our Wat-Coms, the implants tracked their every move. The implants also had miniature cameras to show what the Outsiders could see, and their conversations could always be monitored. We thought it was kind of funny, one of the not-so-bright yet extremely obedient groups at the Complex was called the Monitors. Their job was to constantly be inspecting what people were doing and saying by checking the hundreds of monitors in the viewing rooms and listening randomly to conversations being transmitted through the mini-mics on the Water Closets and implants. We liked to say, "The Monitors monitor the monitors." Well, maybe it wasn't that funny, but in the whole scheme of things, it seemed comical to us.

"What is it like on the Outside?" I signed.

"Well, for one thing, the Outsiders hardly ever wash their hands, maybe only once or twice a day. They don't have washing stations and the washrooms are few and far between," she explained.

"So, how do they not get sick all the time?" I asked. We rarely got sick inside the Complex, since we always used proper precautionary measures and we washed our hands often. I hadn't been sick since I had come to live there, not even once.

"I don't know. It's really weird. It's like they have a resistance to sickness. I mean, lots of Outsiders do get sick a lot, but some of them stay healthy, even though their food isn't real and they practice so many unhealthy habits."

"Yeah, I've seen them on the monitors, touching everyone and eating and drinking all kinds of weird substances, and getting so close to unhealthy people and breathing all over each other. And I've never seen them wash their hands."

"You know, it's not that bad out there," Hiding

Cathy said. "The monitors show some of the worst parts of what's happening on the Outside."

"Really?" I asked. I had just assumed the cameras were capturing a random look at the world Outside the Complex, but it made sense that they would want us to think it was worse on the Outside than it really was, so we would have no desire to leave our safe and happy place of residence.

"It's not as bad as it looks," Hiding Cathy signed, smiling at me.

"What is it really like? I mean, the daily life, the people?"

"The Outsiders are suspicious of people they don't know, but I have kind of blended in, when they've seen me. Most of the time I stay hidden and they don't even notice me, but at times I need to talk to them to get information. They think I'm a relative who risks traveling from my home town to theirs. They think I'm about 10 years old, so they don't suspect me of anything. They have no idea I'm a Kidgen. They think I'm just a person who sneaks from place to place."

"How would you do that if you were an Outsider?"

"They have secret ways of traveling, and people and places that hide travelers, so they think I'm a Sneaker."

"A Sneaker? They think you are a Sneaker?" I giggled.

"That's what they call people who sneak from place to place."

"How far away from the Complex do you go?"

"I go all over the place," she said, shrugging, as if it were no big deal. "Sometimes they send me really far away, but usually they keep me close, so we can track any possible rebellion activities."

"Where do you think we will go on our travel?"

"Well, you know that the only way to get to the Complex from any Outside civilization is by plane, right? We'll have to fly, unless Kenny has some kind of hiking and camping thing set up for us. He could have set up another mode of transportation for us to use. You never know with Kenny. My guess is, I think we will most likely fly."

"No, I didn't know that. I thought we could walk to some places."

She shook her head. "No, it's too far to walk, too dangerous, too much open space where we could be tracked."

I had so many questions. "What about the kids that are Outsiders? What are they like?"

"They play games with each other and most of them live with their parents."

"Really?" I felt a pang of jealousy, a sensation that was extremely unusual to me. At that moment, I missed my life with my parents, my life of so long ago. "I thought, I mean, we know that most of the Outsiders who are parents are addict parents or absent parents."

"There are some of those, but, actually, like I said, the monitors are focused on the worst parts of Outside life. It isn't really as bad out there as they make it seem."

"So, what are the bad parts? What's the down side of Outside life? Besides the food. I know they don't even have the opportunity to eat real food."

"Food is a problem for lots of Outsiders. In some climates, they can grow some of what they eat, and they have all types of fake food, but most Outsiders have a hard time getting enough food. They fight over it, they steal it from each other, and they don't share like they should. Oh, also, whatever they can get, they have to eat it like it is, or they have to cook it themselves. That's where the families have an advantage, because one person can cook for the whole family."

"They don't have an Eatery?" I asked. I had a hard time imagining that. How would they know what to cook? How could they eat the right foods without a Food Manager planning all their meals? Maybe that was why they ate all those non-foods, because, how could they know?

"No, they don't have an Eatery. Each person or each family gets a ration of food when it arrives, and they usually eat it right when they get it, unless they can hide some and eat it later. But there's not really enough food for them to be able to do that. That makes everyone pretty hungry all the time, and they get mean and cranky. Most of them have no patience."

"What about the Chairs? They must have enough food. They are huge!"

"The Chairs are given extra portions of food. They were the ones who had something that the State wanted, so the State promised to take care of them until they die. The State gives the Runners food to take care of the needs of the chairs."

"What do you mean, they had something the State wanted? Like what?"

"They either had weapons or gold or something valuable. When the State confiscated all personal belongings, they were compelled by a huge resistance to give the Holders – that's what they called them back then – to give them some compensation. Since food was the commodity that was so scarce after The Great Devastation, the Holders gladly complied. What good were the weapons if they were going to die of starvation? The State had control of all the food at that time. They had removed every bit of food from every storage site, even from every home."

"Seems like they would have used the weapons to bargain for food," I signed.

"They did. They turned in all the weapons to the State in exchange for being fed for the rest of their lives. Since they were so hungry, they took the deal. Well, most of them did. Some tried to resist and they were killed."

My mouth dropped open. "Killed by the State?"

"Just a few."

"So, how did they become Chairs? Just because they have enough food to eat doesn't mean they have to eat it all at one time."

"They probably feel like they have to eat as much as they can, since the Crims might steal it, or maybe even kill them for it. And, truthfully, I have a notion that the State puts something in their food to make them gain weight, chemicals and additives. Whenever I go on a mission, they warn me not to eat any of the food that the Chairs might offer me." She laughed. "The warning was completely unnecessary because no Chair has ever offered me anything to eat. I take my own food when I go on a mission, and, well, you know, I don't really eat that much."

"Well, you are so small, it doesn't take much for you to get full! What else? Tell me more!" I signed.

"Everyone has to take care of their own hair,"

Hiding Cathy said. "Outside the Complex, they don't have Hair Managers."

"What do you mean?" I asked. "How would I know what to do with this?" I asked, pointing to my mass of curly hair. The Hair Managers knew how to take care of hair and how to make it look nice; thus their title 'Hair Managers.' We didn't have to bother with taking care of our hair.

"Instead of going to a Hair Manager who knows their hair" – she interrupted herself – "who do you go to, anyway?"

"I sometimes go to Rolf Hienemakabottom, but usually I go to Zammie. They are the experts on curly hair. They both do a good job on my hair."

"I like Zammie, too, but I usually go to Sally," Hiding Cathy said. "She's really nice. She is the one who makes my hair so smooth, like this." She tossed her head and her shiny white-blond hair flew out from her head, then each strand settled perfectly back into place.

"Wow, having to think about how to tame my hair all the time would really be a waste of my time," I remarked, feeling sorry for the Outsiders.

"Outside the Complex, they have lots of time," Hiding Cathy said. "But, to look at them, you probably noticed on the monitors, most of them don't really do much with their hair. They just let it be."

"That's weird," I said. "So, do I need to be scared of the Outsiders? I mean, they will know we are not from their village, right? So, will they be suspicious?"

"They might be, but do they have lots of sneakers and wanderers coming through, going from village to village, looking for more food, seeing if anyone has any to spare, which they never do, thanks to the State's rationing program."

"I'm sure Kenrick will make sure we have enough food when we travel," I said. Inside the Complex, we had such an abundance of food, I was sure they were throwing out tons of extra food every day. Our food was not in any way rationed.

"Yeah, we won't have to worry about food," she agreed.

"So, any other significant differences?" I asked. Maybe I should have been asking her what we had in common with the Ordinaries, since everything sounded different.

"Oh, yeah, the Outsiders have to do their own cleaning," she said.

"No way! Oh, man!" I couldn't imagine doing such a disgusting job. I picked up after myself, but to do the actual cleaning was repulsive. That was a job for the Cleaners. "It must be so much worse on the Outside, because they have all that dirt everywhere. They go in and out of buildings all the time, and they spend so much time out of buildings, where it's dirty. So, you're saying they have to clean their own dwellings?"

"Yes, and most of them do not do a good job. Most of the places are really dirty. They hate cleaning, and besides that, they don't have the types of cleaning tools we have. They don't have power all the time, either."

"What do you mean? Solar power is available every day, even when we have the cloud cover."

"They are not set up to receive solar power everywhere. Most villages have only one solar receiving station, and everyone in that village has to share that limited amount of power with the Homes and the dwellings and the hospitals. So, in the dwellings, they get only a few hours of power each day. Oh, there is one thing that is not exaggerated on the monitors. More Ordinaries live in the hospitals than in dwellings or Homes."

"Permanently?" I asked. My heart went out to them, even if they were Ordinaries, because I had heard about the crowded conditions of the hospitals.

"Most of them. And they have so few people to take care of them, it's like a big place for sick and injured people to go and be sick. Most of them never recover, once they go into a hospital. They might stay there a week or a few months, although I have my theories about that, too. The ones in the hospitals are drugged beyond recognition, to keep them quiet, to keep them in their beds, so the few caretakers can handle their huge loads."

"Doesn't sound like they are very good caretakers," I said, making a face.

"Imagine this. You are a caretaker – I know, we are not that type, but just imagine – you are a caretaker and you are responsible to take care of three hundred people every day."

"Wouldn't they want some of the sick people to get better so they can help take care of the other sick ones?"

"Only the people who have already been identified as caretaker types can help. The rest, they keep them drugged until they die, or are put to sleep forever. Well, most of them, anyway. Some of the injured, if their injuries are not too bad, they help them get better, that is, when they have enough food. Even the hospitals are low on food most of the time. The Outside population is really decreasing rapidly."

"The State wants the Outside population to decrease, because, from what they tell us, life would be so much better if we only had the Insiders, but we don't have enough room for everyone to live inside the Complex."

"That is not really true. It's just more Prop. They don't want to lose all the Outsiders," Hiding Cathy told me. "They use the Outsiders to do things for the State, things we can't do from the Inside, like grow food and animals," Hiding Cathy explained.

"It's a lot worse than I imagined on the Outside," I said, slightly disappointed.

"It's worse in some ways, but better in other ways. The Ordinaries are not constantly monitored unless they have been identified as a threat, and the Crims are really subdued, due to the transmissions they receive in their implants. So, the Ordinaries can talk about anything, at any time. They even have groups that gather to worship God."

"Are you serious?" Worshipping God was strictly forbidden in the Complex. We were not allowed to acknowledge, even in our own minds, that God existed. I was glad they couldn't fully control our minds, regardless of their methods of manipulation.

"They don't even stop them. And the kids, the Ordinaries, get to play whenever they want. They don't have to work. Their parents teach them at home. The kids play with each other. They run around by themselves, without any adult supervision, and they have all kinds of games that they play."

I remembered, a flash of a memory, when my parents taught me at home, and I played with other kids and with my parents. No matter what the State told us, I knew parents were good, beneficial, and, actually, wonderful. My heart ached for my parents at that moment, but I wasn't sure if I really wanted to mingle among the Ordinaries. I wondered what exactly Kenrick was planning for our travel.

"What about your parents?" I asked her. "What happened to them, if you don't mind me asking?"

"My mother died when I was very young, and my father is here, at the Complex."

"Really?" I asked. She still got to see her father? "Who is he? Where does he work?"

"He is one of the Food Managers, but he does a lot of traveling. He makes deals for food with the Ordinaries, and he arranges for the deliveries. He goes all kinds of places to get food for us to eat here at the Complex."

"Have I ever met him, do you think?"

"I doubt it," she said sadly. "I don't even get to see him very often, maybe once every few months. We have to meet in secret and when we see each other in public, we have to pretend that we are not related. I haven't seen him in a long time."

"That's terrible!" I said. Would it be worse for a young girl to never see her parents, or to be so limited in visiting them that they had to pretend they didn't know each other? At least I had no expectation that I would ever see my parents, so I would not be disappointed, nor did I have to pretend. And what was this kind of special permission that she had, to be able to lie to everyone about her family status? If I were in her situation, I would not be able to contain myself; I would have to give my dad a hug, especially if I only saw him once a month.

"Are you going to go eat?" Hiding Cathy asked aloud.

"I could eat," I answered. I was feeling quite hungry. "I would love to have some more of those stuffed grape leaves."

"They were so good!" Hiding Cathy agreed, nodding excitedly.

"Let's go see what they are offering at the Eatery," I suggested.

"I'm ready!" she said, jumping off the bed.

I went into the washroom to change out of my sleeper. I was amazed at how small Hiding Cathy was. I was also amazed that she had chosen me to be her close friend. She seemed to be afraid of everyone, but she didn't act frightened around me. I knew I presented no threat to her, but who did, in the Complex? We were all perfectly safe inside the Complex. The real question was, how did she survive outside the Complex? That's where things could get scary. Maybe if I could hide as well as Hiding Cathy did, I wouldn't be afraid on the Outside either.

As we walked across the Complex to the Eatery, Kenrick whooshed past us, moving so quickly that I knew he was a mere blur on the monitors. He breathed one word between Hiding Cathy and myself that we felt rather than heard: "Tomorrow."

CHAPTER 3

As I sat at my workstation, I was so nervous; yet I had to appear as if everything were absolutely normal. I saw Big Hawk across the room while I was working, and he was not betraying any type of emotion. He looked as if he were merely doing his job and this was just another normal day with nothing outstanding about to happen. I glanced at everyone else in the room... could they tell we had an escape plan? Would we actually be able to get away today, or would we be caught and punished? We were well aware of what the range of punishments could be. If they decided that we were only going 'out to play' we would be burdened with more work and not allowed to see each other for some yet-to-be-determined period of time. If they figured that we were going to travel, like we were planning, and they knew it had been pre-planned, we could have some solitary confinement and more work. However, if they concluded we were in any way trying to betray the State or compromise the security of our work there, we could be sent Outside the Complex for good, labeled as Crims, and our foreheads implanted. We knew the risk we were taking, and we also knew it was entirely possible for us to get away from the Complex, take our travel, come back, (get our Wat-Coms from the cow), without getting caught, and come back to work, as if our time Outside had been legally authorized, with no penalty in any way. That was our plan. That was our goal.

For a moment I wondered how Kenrick had taken care of everything he needed to do to get us out of the Complex in just one day. Then I realized that he had been planning it for a long time, and, for his safety and ours, he hadn't told us about his extra in-depth activities and schemes until the last minute. I tried to imagine all the details he had covered without anyone knowing: giving each of us clearance to leave the Complex; programming our WCs so the Gate Guards would think we had permission to leave, and so alarms wouldn't be triggered when we stepped outside the Wall; distributing our workloads to others while we were gone (however long that would be, only Kenrick knew at this point); as well as providing a wardrobe for us for when we were Outside. We wouldn't be safe walking around in our Complex outfits or even our uniforms without any security guards to protect us... or had he even scheduled guards to go with us? He probably had to do a lot of other things that I didn't even know anything about. I didn't doubt anything he did; he knew so much and he had access to every computer system... and they had absolutely no idea what we were going to do! If they knew, we would not be allowed to be working so normally at our workspaces; we would be shunned for a day or a week and would not be allowed to see each other or partake in any type of entertainment until our punishment ended. The fact that we were allowed to be carrying on with our usual duties confirmed that they didn't know anything about our secret plans; and with Kenrick's manipulating and maneuvering, I hoped they never would know anything about our little escapade.

I wondered what we would eat while we were on the Outside. Surely, Kenrick would have something great prepared for us to take with us. We couldn't be expected to eat the kinds of imitation food the Outsiders ate. I thought about the cashew chicken dish I had eaten the night before, and the bread-bowl soup Hiding Cathy had had. How could we possibly eat anything outside the Complex? I had never heard about anyone on the Outside having access to real food. Their drink that I couldn't understand was soda pop: artificially colored, artificially flavored, artificially sweetened, artificially bubbled water; and the Ordinaries and the Chairs and the Crims drank it as if it were the best thing in the world! That didn't make any sense to me. No wonder they were stuck with such low intelligent factors, and so many were sick all the time. They didn't get any nutrition from their intake! However, since I never planned to taste soda pop, I wouldn't ever have to suffer the consequences of drinking it.

I was so glad I was already finished with my work. Some of us Kidgens had an expression we liked to use: "I work so fast, I'm always finished." They were constantly giving me puzzles and codes that they thought were more and more difficult, but with my gift, I could just look at them and instantly see the patterns. When they were in different languages it sometimes took a few minutes, but since my dad had taught me five languages before I was even five years old, even the languages were part of my nature. I secretly liked the codes in other languages that were given to me; they were like a special hidden connection to my dad. I didn't dare tell anyone about it, but I held it inside my mind and especially in my heart. When I decoded the messages, I could almost hear my dad's voice, from so long ago, speaking the words in that foreign language to me.

I had finished my mandatory outdoor time by roller skating ten times around the full loop of the walkway that went around Complex. While skating, I felt so free, able to move so fast and feel the breeze on my face, blowing back my hair. I loved to stretch my legs and do all kinds of dancing skate moves. I imagined that some of the Monitors were watching me on the monitors, and I wanted to entertain them. They probably weren't really watching me, but just in case they were, I wanted to give them something fun to watch, a performance. I skated forwards and backwards and pretended like I was skiing down a slope, with both feet parallel as I moved from side to side on the walkway. It was a little bit unusual to not meet anyone else on the walkway, but some days I was the only one taking my mandatory outdoor time at that time. I was glad for the break, to keep anyone from hearing my heart thumping so loudly as I sat at my workstation, daydreaming about our upcoming travel. I was hoping Kenrick scheduled it to happen soon, because I was sure my friends had to be as distracted as I was.

I had just changed out of my skates and into my shoes, and I was sitting at my workstation wondering what to do next, since I didn't have any more assigned work. I decided to go over to watch the monitors for awhile. We were encouraged to look in on the monitors when we were not working, just to add extra sets of eyes to keep track of what was happening, both inside the Complex and on the Outside. I was interested at this time at what might be happening Outside. I had a whole new reason and interest to observe the monitors, since I would soon be Outside. I wanted to see the things the Ordinaries were seeing; I might soon be doing the things they were doing. The trick was, I had to behave as if I had the same lack of interest in the Outside activities as I always did, as we always did.

I went into the Monitor Cave – we called it a cave because it was so dark inside, but it was officially called the Viewing Room – where every wall was covered with monitors that were labeled with their viewing locations. I had been in there many times before, but then it was only for amusement or entertainment. This time I was there for information, education, so I could discover what types of people I might need to interact with, or protect myself from; or avoid completely.

The seats of the Monitors who worked there were filled, as they sat, staring. From my vantage point behind them, I couldn't tell who was awake and working and watching, and who was sleeping, but I didn't really care about that. I was glad no one acknowledged my presence as I slipped into the first section of the Monitor Cave.

Some of the screens were showing sections of the Complex, inside and out, where the signal changed every 15 seconds to a new view. We never knew exactly when we were on camera, so we were always prepared to be viewed at all times. Only in some areas of our pods did we have some privacy, and even there the audio bugs were all over the place, in addition to the mics in our Wat-Coms. I quickly scanned the monitors and I didn't find anything in this section that was worth watching. I saw the Eatery, our workstations, the indoor fountains, the path around the Complex, the swimming pool, the hair managing station and the clothing station, where we got our clothes. For a few moments I focused on the camera that was on the front gate, the one we would very soon be passing through, but the Gate Guards were just standing around talking to each other. No one was going in or out, so there wasn't anything for me to see there. I moved to the next section of screens in the Monitor Cave, beyond where I usually looked.

Now, there was something interesting. There was a group of monitors with the label "Crims" on them. How could they know only Crims would be in that vicinity? A group of Crims was standing in a yard, about 15 or so of them, and there were several cameras showing them from different angles. Even if the monitors had not been labeled, I could tell they were Crims by their extra large scars on their foreheads, where they had their implants, and by the clothing they were required to wear, a canary yellow type of outfit that could easily be spotted in the crowds. I wondered what they were doing. I watched them for a minute and I observed that they weren't doing anything. They were just standing there. They weren't talking to each other. I focused my attention on their faces, because something was not right about them. They all had odd expressions. I stepped a little closer to the monitors, being careful to not draw any attention to myself, to see what could possibly be going on with them.

As I looked more closely, I could see it, the difference. They all had dull eyes. Their eyelids looked heavy, and they had no spark of life in them, even though some of them were younger than I was. My first thought was that they were drugged; but how would that make any sense, since most of them were Crims because of drugs. Then, as I stood watching them closely as they did nothing and had absolutely no ambition, I knew they were being controlled by their implants. The way they all moved their arms, ever so slightly, and then they all brushed back an invisible strand of hair in unison, as if they had practiced this a thousand times, told me that they were all receiving signals in their brains, signals that controlled even their involuntary movements. They were under complete control of a programmer or, actually, a puppeteer, who was pulling their strings! I could imagine some guy sitting at his computer, pushing buttons and speaking commands and laughing as he watched them move together like a group of synchronized swimmers. Well, I didn't need to be afraid of the Crims. They obviously couldn't even leave that yard unless they received a signal from central command. I moved to the next group of monitors, the one labeled "Chairs."

I hadn't really paid any attention to this group before. The monitors were very dark, showing scenes inside rooms, and it was difficult for me to see anything. As I was able to barely distinguish what was happening on one of the monitors, my heart cried and I had to stifle my reaction.

I could see an enormous person in a large, comfortable chair. That much, I expected. What shocked me was the small person who was also in the room, obviously one of the Runners, who was poking and taunting and teasing the Chair; or, as I chose at that moment, and from them on, to call him, the Person in the Chair. Our society had reduced him, that person, and others like him, to just being a piece of furniture that could never leave his house. He was way too big to fit through the door, so a Runner had been assigned to take care of his needs, to bring his food and pick up his remote control if he dropped it. But this Runner was not taking care of this person in the chair at all – he was hurting him! I could see, although the room was very dark, I could see the glistening of tears on the person's face. I assumed it was a man in the chair, but it was so dark I couldn't tell. It could have been a woman. Whoever he or she was, this Person in the Chair was very unhappy, and the Runner was just dancing around the chair that contained the person and laughing.

I glanced around at the Monitors who were employed to be monitoring the monitors, and they seemed to be aware yet unconcerned that this Runner was teasing this poor person. I was appalled to watch as the Runner held out a plate of food, then snatched it away from the Person in the Chair. This person was not a chair! Maybe he had to live in a chair, but he was a human who was being treated as if he had no importance, no worth!

I felt a stab of guilt as I considered the fact that we Insiders considered ourselves to be so much better than the Crims and the Persons in the Chairs and the Runners and the Ordinaries, simply because we lived Inside the Complex. How were we any better than they were, if we were aware of this mistreating of humans and we just let it continue to happen, without stopping it, or even caring that it was happening?

I focused in on another Person in a Chair on a different monitor. I saw a very large young woman, very beautiful, reaching, reaching, trying to reach something that she had dropped. She had no Runner in the room with her, and she was leaning over the side of her chair, trying to get something. I could see that she was sweating. She was crying! Her red light was on, indicating that she had already signaled for a Runner to come and help her, but there she was, all alone and unable to take care of her own needs. I wondered how long she had been waiting? I wondered how far away from us she was? Could I somehow help her? Why didn't anyone seem to care about these people? I had heard the Prop, that it was their own fault because they ate everything they wanted to eat, but was it really their fault? Had they had been made that way by the supplements they were given to eat or did their implants manipulate the portion of their brains that controlled their weight and body shape? If they could control the Crims by their implants, they certainly could control the eating habits and the body metabolism of the Persons they chose to put in the Chairs. After seeing the people on the monitors, I could no longer believe that the Persons in the Chairs had put themselves there. I observed monitor after monitor of Persons in Chairs. Some were sleeping. Some were watching their screens, looking like they were mildly interested. Some were eating. A few were crying.

I didn't want to watch the Persons in the Chairs any more. I knew I would never forget what I had just seen, but what could I do about it? I didn't even know where they were, or where their village was. These scenes could be anywhere! I hoped Kenrick would be taking us on our travel to see some of these people, these real, live people, who had been dismissed by the State. I somehow felt more of a connection to the Outsiders than the Insiders; not that I was ready to give up my status, but I had to think of something I could do to help all those people who were being so horribly mistreated.

I moved to the next set of monitors, which were brightly lit and full of sunshine, and I saw some of the Ordinaries in what must have been a park. The scene was inviting. Children were running, playing a game. Adults were laughing and conversing nearby. One of the little girls ran over to a lady that was obviously her mother – they had the same blond, curly hair and wide smiles with shining teeth. The mother turned from the group of adults and she squatted down to be on the same level as her daughter. She brushed a lock of hair off of the little girl's brow as she listened to what the child had to say. The mother nodded and smiled at the child, and kissed her forehead. The little girl scampered off to play with her friends again.

Now my heart was aching for another reason. In some far corner of my mind, I could recall my own mother doing the same thing for me: she gave me all of her attention to listen to my own little problem, one that was the biggest problem in the world for me at that time, and then she helped me solve the problem and she even added a kiss on my forehead. I couldn't let anyone in the Complex know, but I really missed my mother. Could I find her on one of these monitors?

I turned away from the groups of happy families and I went deeper into the Monitor Cave to the monitors labeled 'Homes.' My mother was in one of those places and I had seen her there, when she had been either unconscious or barely conscious. Had I been somehow programmed to not even want to see her? I didn't know where she was. Until now, it had not occurred to me to search for her on the monitors.

The scenes on these monitors were also very dark. I could get glimpses of room after room of somebody sleeping in a bed, unattended and unmoving. If one of these persons were my mom, I had no way of knowing. They all looked about the same, except in one room where there were two people standing near the bed. I was curious as to what they might be doing, so I took a closer look. One person leaned over and looked at the sleeper, then the other person did the same thing. From this angle, I couldn't see the sleeper's face, just the back of his or her body which was covered with a blanket, and the back of the head, which was covered with messed-up hair. Both of the people in the room, I couldn't tell if they were men or women, since the room was so dark, leaned over at the same time and appeared to be closely examining the sleeper. Then they both stepped back, away from the bed and they looked at each other. One of them took something off the counter behind them while the other person watched. They kind of fumbled with something, then I watched in horror as one person stuck a huge needle into the sleeper's arm, waited a few seconds, then withdrew the needle. They both moved quickly and gathered up some things that were scattered about the room. They hurried out of the room and closed the door behind them. Who were those people, and what authority did they have to give that sleeping person an injection? Where they family members or did they work there? Or were they enemies of the sleeper?

At this point, I was convinced that the real-life happenings on the monitors were far more interesting to watch than any of the fiction movies we were allowed to view! I was upset, so upset that I couldn't bear to stay and watch the monitors any longer. I had never seen that much action on the monitors before, but, then, I had never looked at them for so long or with such diligence. I didn't like what I had just seen. Reality was not pretty.

I left the Monitor Cave and tried to think of something to do. I was finished with my work, so I had no reason to return to my workstation. I was too upset to eat anything, so I had no desire to go to the Eatery. I had already finished with my mandatory outdoor time, and I was nicely exhausted from my earlier skating rounds. The Entertainment Module didn't sound interesting at this time. What did I want to do? I wanted to find Hiding Cathy and talk to her about what I had just seen. What did she know about those situations? Had she seen the terrible conditions and treatment of the Persons in the Chairs when she had gone on her missions? Were all Runners as cruel as the one I observed on the monitor?

I sat by the fountain and sent a message via my Wat-Com to Hiding Cathy to meet me there. As I waited, the anticipation of our travel returned, although it had been slightly dampened by the disturbing scenes I had just witnessed. I was kind of angry with myself, because these awful things were probably happening all the time, and I had just been living as if my charmed lifestyle were the only one that was in any way important. I had been living for so long in ignorant bliss... yet, really, deep inside, hadn't I known that life was not fair, and that we at the Complex were given special treatment every day of our lives? I did know that, and I had been taking it all for granted, without any sympathy for the Ordinaries and the other Outsiders and all the problems they had to face on a daily basis.

Where was Hiding Cathy, anyway? Why wasn't she responding to my message? We always sent each other a quick reply as soon as we received a communication from the other.

Several Kidgens walked by me and we acknowledged each other as they passed. I had seen them before – they were working on a special project for the State, some kind of security database program, and they were setting up the wireless access points for the new systems. I knew they were really smart, but all of their intelligence combined didn't even approach the knowledge and wisdom Kenrick had. Every Kidgen as well as every Comgen at the Complex dreamed of someday being as smart as Kenrick, but he had just been born with his gift. The genius gene was firmly rooted in him and his range of understanding grew by leaps and bounds every day. I wasn't jealous of him; I was very glad that he was my friend, and that we were close friends.

The four of us – Kenrick, Big Hawk, Hiding Cathy and I – had naturally become good friends shortly after we met at the Complex. We had become a group of friends, and although we knew other Kidgens and Comgens, none of the others clicked together with us like we did. It was as if we were destined to become friends, as if we had been made for each other. We all had different skills and different strengths, and we complimented each other when we worked together, but our bond was more than that. We truly liked each other. We were drawn to each other and we enjoyed spending time together. We sometimes invited others to join us in activities, but no one else really fit together with us the way we did with each other. I counted it a blessing to have three best friends, and that's what we called each other, secretly. At the Complex, they wanted no one to have any preference over any other person for any reason, but they just couldn't control our hearts, and our hearts wanted us to be together. We just had to act casual at all times, but we knew each other so well, we could secretly say we all four loved each other as family.

Thinking about my friends temporarily took my mind off the disturbing scenes on the monitors and I again became giddy with anticipation of our travel. Kenrick had said we would be traveling today! The four of us soon would be leaving the Complex and going somewhere on the Outside together!

CHAPTER 4

I got a buzz on my Wat-Com from Hiding Cathy. She said she would meet me at the fountain in a few minutes; she had been asleep. How could she sleep on a day like this? Wasn't her heart beating a thousand beats per second like mine was? Or was this merely another journey for her? But she was always so scared, wouldn't she be afraid now? Or maybe that was all a front, maybe she was just acting scared all the time as part of her character. That didn't seem likely, since she was apt to be under a table or desk or chair in a flash, out of sight before anyone realized she was gone; but perhaps it was all part of her craft. We all had specific skills that had given us entrance to the Complex. Mine was finding patterns and hers was hiding herself.

I stared into the fountain and I had to force myself to not see and try to decode the water patterns. Of course the water was falling in patterns, it was coming out of the fountainhead in patterns and falling logically from one point to the other, its destination. So, why did it seem to be spelling out a message to me? What was it saying? As I looked at the water patterns, trying to break my stare, I could see an obvious code in the falling water. It said, in so many ways, 'Open.' I could see code, as plain as day. But what did it mean? Who would put a message in the water fountain? Was this another programming ploy of Kenrick's? The message was so obvious, I was afraid other people would see it and suspect something. Several of the Programmers walked by the fountain and they didn't even pay any attention to me or the blatant secret message.

My supervisor was approaching me. Oh, no, what if he knew something? I had to stay cool. I couldn't let him see the code! He might guess that we were going to walk through the open gate and go into the open world today!

"Did you eat yet?" he asked.

I was so relieved, I couldn't think of what to say to him.

"What?" I asked, trying to behave as if this were just another ordinary day.

"I asked if you have eaten yet," he said patiently. Was he saying it too patiently? What was going on with him? Was he suspicious?

"I ate earlier, much earlier, but I haven't eaten lately," I said, trying to be nonchalant.

"Well, if you haven't eaten lately, you should eat soon," he said. He seemed to be looking through me.

"Yes, that is a good idea," I said. "I will."

"Great," he said, nodding slowly. "You don't want to get too hungry."

"No, I don't," I replied. I forced a smile.

"Are you waiting for somebody?" he asked, looking suddenly distracted.

"Yes, as a matter of fact, I am," I said.

"Well, good luck with that," he said, then he headed off toward the Entertainment Module, leaving me to wonder about his motivation for that interaction. I watched him as he walked through the Complex. Obviously his mind was elsewhere, and that was fine with me. I didn't want him to take any interest in me, especially at that time.

Hiding Cathy was all of a sudden beside me.

"Oh, you scared me!" I said, startled.

"What are you doing?" she asked. "What's the matter?" Hiding Cathy was as calm as anyone had ever been. She looked unusually refreshed from her nap.

"Um, nothing," I said, trying to decide where to start: what I had seen on the monitors, or the message in the fountain, or my supervisor's odd behavior.

"Something is going on," she said, scanning our surroundings. I recognized she meant that something was going on in the Complex. My first thought was that whatever it was might delay our travel!

"What are you talking about?" I asked. We knew from experience that we could converse quietly near the fountain and our voices couldn't be heard over the sound of the water.

"I'm not sure, but we better stay alert," Hiding Cathy said.

"Look at the fountain," I said.

Obediently, she looked, but I could see that she couldn't see what I could see.

"It's almost hypnotizing," she said, staring at it.

"Do you see anything strange?" I asked, looking for a clue on her face.

"I see a lot of water being recycled, pumped from down there to up there and back again," she said. She couldn't see the message, yet it was so clear!

"You don't see anything strange?" I asked again.

"Nothing is strange," she said. "Everything is normal." She nodded her head, still looking at the water.

Was she teasing me, or did she have to say that because of the monitors?

"I can see a message in there," I said quietly, not

letting my lips move as I spoke.

"Of course you can," Hiding Cathy said. "You see messages everywhere."

I was about to reply to that comment when I got a buzz on my Wat-Com from Kenrick. I could tell Hiding Cathy got one, too, at the same time. I wondered if all the Insiders were staring at us as we made our way across the Complex to the Eatery, but they all appeared to simply be doing their work, as if this were just another normal day, which, for them, it was. For my three friends and me, it was our first day of our clandestine adventure!

We met Kenrick and Big Hawk, washed our hands, got our meals and sat at one of the less visible tables, back near the kitchen door where it was generally noisy. We knew how hard it was to hear conversation over the monitors when people were sitting in that area, and with the odd way Kenrick pronounced his words and spoke so quickly, even we often had a hard time understanding him when we were right there with him and looking at him.

"Everything is set," he told us, as he took a big bite of his spinach pie. That was a great extra added precaution – we had to struggle to decipher his sentences while his mouth was full. "Don't go back to your pods. When we finish eating, we will walk out the East Entrance and go around the path to the Exit Gate. Just act normal, don't look around and stuff, just walk out with authority. I have given us all top clearance authority."

"Don't we need–" Hiding Cathy began.

"Everything we need is waiting for us," Kenrick interrupted. "It's all prepared. Don't question, don't worry."

I still had a million questions, but I knew better than to ask any of them then. We would have plenty of time for talking when we were out of range, after we attached our Wat-Coms to a cow's leg. I smiled at the thought. Were we actually going to do that? It sounded ridiculous but it was thrilling!

We ate our meals with some light conversation. We put our trays on the counter and washed our hands. My heart was thudding with excitement and I was trying to control its beating so it wouldn't betray us through my Wat-Com pulse monitor. We walked together through the Complex to the East Entrance, the same way we had done thousands of times. I felt eyes watching us, but my logic was working to convince me that they trusted us. They had no idea what we were doing. We were just kids who were going outside the Complex, inside the Wall, for a break. Then, there we were, out in the open, outside the building but inside the Wall, where every inch of space was covered by cameras. The Monitors who monitored the Outside monitors were more diligent than the rest of the Monitors. We had to behave the same way we always did, pretending to laugh and converse about nothing important. This time, though, we didn't stand around looking at the fountains or go sit on a bench by one of the manufactured gardens. We stayed on the path to the exit gate, as if we had clearance to leave. I had to keep in mind, we DID have clearance to leave; Kenrick had given it to us, free and clear.

As we approached the Exit Gate, I used my breathing techniques so in my highly excited condition I wouldn't arouse the suspicion of the Gate Guards. The Gate Guards weren't paying any attention to us, though, for some reason. All four of them were entranced by their Wat-Coms. I glanced at mine and saw that nothing out of the ordinary was being displayed as we walked through the detectors. No alarms were sounded and the Gate Guards didn't even acknowledge our presence, an extremely odd occurrence. They didn't stop us. As I understood, they were to scan our IDs, ask us where we were going and how long we would be gone, and check our clearance in the computer. They didn't say anything to us. Kenrick was in the lead and he said something to them that I couldn't understand. They didn't respond to him. They didn't seem to even notice we were there, walking out of the Complex. We walked right out of the Complex!

We followed Kenrick straight down the road without talking. I had a hard time just walking and not dancing down the road, I was so excited. I forced my feet to keep a steady pace. When we had walked for about 20 minutes and were well out of sight of the Complex, safely away without having been stopped, Kenrick nodded to Hiding Cathy. She pointed to a path off to the left, and we followed it for quite some time. I saw a large building ahead of us in the distance. We approached the building and Hiding Cathy stopped and looked at the wall. She put her hand into a space that I hadn't noticed and a small door opened in front of her. She beckoned for us to quickly follow her inside the building. Kenrick was right behind Hiding Cathy. Just as Big Hawk ducked his head to enter after me, the door closed.

My eyes took a few seconds to adjust to the dark, and during that time I smelled an awful odor, a strong odor that I did not recognize. Before I could see anything, I knew where we were: we had found Hiding Cathy's cow! Actually, once I could see, I became aware that there were lots of cows in the building, cows that were not paying any attention to what we were doing. Who fed these cows, I wondered. Hiding Cathy took us over to an area where some brown and white cows were in a pen. She took off her Wat-Com and motioned for us to do the same, as she attached hers to the leg of one of the cows. I had never removed mine! It was forbidden! I had been wearing it since they gave it to me, nearly nine years ago. I wasn't even sure how to unhook it so I could get it off my wrist, but Kenrick and Big Hawk had taken off theirs in a flash. Hiding Cathy reached over to my wrist and somehow unclasped my WC and in one motion she reconnected it on the cow's leg. Then she switched on a small machine that was near the cow's pen and she motioned for us to follow her out of the building, through another door on the other side of the building. She pointed to four backpacks that were propped up near the exit, and we each grabbed one as we were going out the door. I slung mine over my shoulders, and the others did the same with theirs.

When we were out in the sunlight again, my eyes flickered as they adjusted to the brightness. My friends began chattering about our new and forbidden freedom, but I saw it: a tree! It was a real, living, growing tree! I had no idea any trees were growing so close to the Complex! Ignoring my friends, I ran over to the tree and inhaled its beautiful scent. The trunk was enormous – it must have been hundreds of years old! I looked up, straight up, and I noticed how it seemed to poke the sky. How could I not have seen this tree as we approached the building? I glanced around at our surroundings.

I hadn't seen the small hill near the building. When we went in the building, we were on one side of the hill, and when we came out of the building, we were on the other side of the hill. I tried to hug the huge tree, which, at this part of the trunk, was at least eight feet in diameter, and all kinds of little sticks and sticker things poked my hands and arms. I smelled it as much as possible and tried to memorize the pattern of its beautiful bark. I saw no message in this pattern, just magnificence. I stepped back a few steps to look up at the millions of leaves above my head. They were not all the same shade of green, but a wide variety of greens, each one delicately and intricately painted. I marveled at the majesty of this lone tree.

I returned to my friends. I had been so excited about the tree, I had been missing their conversation.

"This hill blocks the transmissions," Hiding Cathy was explaining.

"But the signals go to satellites," Big Hawk said. "How can a small hill block anything from going to outer space?"

"There is some kind of mineral inside the hill that makes the signals go wacky," Hiding Cathy said. "That's why I turned on that scrambler by the cows. It sends a signal so the monitors will hear sounds that make them think we're talking."

"All of us?" I asked. "Our voices?"

"Yeah, sorry I couldn't let you guys know, I recorded some of our conversations," Kenrick said. "I put them on a chip and Hiding Cathy put it in the scrambler. It will generate random conversations until we come back."

I didn't care. Probably all of our conversations were recorded anyway. "What if someone finds it?" I asked.

"The farmers know they are not to bother the cows in the last pen," Hiding Cathy said. "That area is off limits to them. If they enter, an alarm will send a signal and they will be in big trouble."

"Then why could we–" I began, then I understood. "Kenrick, you did it, didn't you?"

"I just did what I had to do to keep us safe," he said, shrugging his shoulders.

"You did something to the Gate Guards, too, huh?" Big Hawk asked, smiling and nodding his head.

"What?" I asked. "What did you do? Why did they just ignore us like that? They are suppose to check every person, scan the ID and match the picture with what they have on record, check the clearance, and they didn't do any of that! They just ignored us, like we weren't even there."

"I just gave them something very interesting to watch," Kenrick said, with a chuckle. "A convenient distraction, something extremely compelling." I thought about the Crims, how they had been acting when I had recognized their brains were being programmed.

"I bet you did," Big Hawk said, his giant grin stretching across his face.

"Where are we going now?" I asked, looking around at this interesting landscape. I was so curious, so excited! It did not really matter to me where we were going. We were already there, as far as I was concerned, away from the Complex, on a secret adventure!

"Just a little jaunt," Kenrick said mysteriously. He started walking, and we followed him.

"I feel weird without my Wat-Com," I said. My wrist felt so incredibly naked, I rubbed it with my other hand.

"Do you want to go back and get it?" Big Hawk asked, pausing, as if to return to the barn building.

"No, thanks, we'll get them soon enough," I said. "I was just remarking that I feel weird without it. I have never taken it off, ever since I got it."

"Never?" Kenrick asked.

"No, why? Have you?" I asked.

"No," Kenrick and Big Hawk said in unison, as they exchanged glances. I didn't believe them. How could they have known how to take them off so quickly?

We were following Kenrick down a long path out in nowhere. I didn't see any signs of civilization or even nature ahead of us. I guess I was expecting to find an off-limits forest or a lake or something, but all we saw was a path across the plain, with some little bushes all over the place.

"How long are we going to be gone?" Hiding Cathy asked. For some reason, I had one week in my mind, but Kenrick wasn't going to give up any information to us yet.

"We'll see," was all he would tell us.

"Okay, so, you won't tell us where we're going," Big Hawk said. "Where do they think we are?"

"Well…" Kenrick began, "they don't know we are together. We each have a different assignment, we are not on a pleasure cruise and we are not visiting family."

That made me think that maybe we WOULD be visiting family, and maybe I would be able to see my mom again. I didn't know her location, but I was sure Kenrick knew, or he could find out where she was. He usually had several portable devices with him at all times, and he could access anything from anywhere.

"Shh!" Hiding Cathy said, quickly and quietly. We all froze in our tracks. I thought I had sensed something also. We were caught! We would be punished! With the backpacks on us, I knew our plans would seem to be very devious to anyone who found us, and thus warrant severe penalty.

A bush near us trembled ever so slightly. Any type of device could be hidden in it; or a small spy like Hiding Cathy could be concealed there. I didn't dare move a muscle. I wondered if my pounding heartbeat could be detected?

Hiding Cathy moved swiftly and a rabbit hopped out of the bush and very quickly scampered across the plain. We burst into laughter, and I realized how nervous I really was about this whole thing. I was nearly terrified that we would be caught. But it was too late to turn back. We were on our way to somewhere else.

"I decided to make all of our assignments covert so no one can ask us about them when we go back," Kenrick said.

"Great idea!" Hiding Cathy exclaimed.

"Will we have to report to a Superior?" Big Hawk asked.

"Ahh, that's the beauty of the plan," Kenrick said. "Our assignments are so covert, no one has clearance to see who ordered the assignments, or who we are responsible to. Everyone will just see that we are on assignments, and no one can see who approved for us to go, and they can't see our specific assignments. They won't be allowed to ask us any questions."

"Kenny, you are so smart!" Hiding Cathy squealed.

"That's because I'm a Kidgen and a Comgen," Kenny stated. He wasn't bragging, he was merely stating a fact. He was smarter than any of the adults we worked with, even the Superiors, because no one else had such a grasp on the workings of the computers and the systems. He didn't have to hack into any of the systems – he was the master programmer of all of them. Nobody else knew what he knew, although they were trying to find someone for him to train to be his understudy. I couldn't think of any suitable persons at our Complex who could even begin to do what Kenrick could so easily do, and our Complex was supposed to have the brightest of the bright.

"This is my first time leaving the Complex." I admitted.

"Since when?" Big Hawk asked. I craned my neck to look up at him and I could see how he lived up to his name: his eyes were scanning the horizon, as if searching for prey.

"Since I came to live there," I said. The time had really just run together and it didn't seem like years and years since I had been Outside the Complex.

"I thought you visited your mother?" Hiding Cathy said.

"That was before I came to live there," I explained. Why was she mentioning my mother? Were we going to see her?

"We need to change out of our uniforms now," Kenrick said, stepping over to a larger small bush. He pointed to a small bin that was hidden by the bush. "In your backpack is a change of clothes. Put your uniforms in this bin." He began to unbutton his shirt as I took off my backpack and unzipped it. I pulled out an enormous shirt.

"I think I got yours," Big Hawk and I said to each other, at the same time.   We exchanged backpacks and I went behind another bush near where Hiding Cathy was, to change my clothes. Kenrick had chosen some smart casuals for us to wear, like nothing else I had. Some Insiders had their own sets of casuals, but I had no need for them. I had my uniforms for work, my cozy clothes for relaxing at my pod or enjoying entertainment and my sleepers, and I didn't need anything else to wear. These clothes were appealing as well as comfortable, and Kenrick had furnished the perfect sizes for each of us. Everyone back at the Complex really underestimated him, due to his lack of communicating with them socially, but we, his friends, knew he was capable of doing anything he wanted to do – and even a lot of things he didn't want to do.

"Where are our scars?" Hiding Cathy asked, digging through her backpack.

"Yeah, don't we need to wear fake scars?" I asked, as if I were so experienced in this area. I never would have thought of it if Hiding Cathy hadn't mentioned it to me during our conversation.

"We won't be needing them," Kenrick said.

"We have to have them!" Hiding Cathy said. "Without a scar, the Ordinaries will know we're not one of them. We won't be able to blend in if we don't have scars."

"Yeah," Big Hawk agreed. "They will turn us in immediately. And when the Monitors see us on the monitors, we will be caught and we'll be in big trouble."

"We won't be seen," Kenrick said.

"How can we not be seen?" I asked, putting on my backpack again. "There are cameras everywhere."

"In every established area there are cameras,"

Kenrick corrected.

"You mean we're not going–" Hiding Cathy began.

"That's right," Kenrick said, nodding in an exaggerated manner, as if that explained everything.

"What are you saying?" I asked, as we continued walking down the path.

"We are going to places," Kenrick said mysteriously, "where there is no civilization."

"Places where there is no civilization?" I echoed.

"Places? Plural?" Big Hawk asked. "How many places are we going to be going?"

"Three places," Kenrick said.

"Three? Three places? We are going to three places?" I asked excitedly. "Three places where there is no civilization? Where are they? Where are we going?"

"I'm not saying another word until the time is right," Kenrick said.

I had no idea where we could possibly be going. I didn't know what kinds of places were available for us to visit; but then, Kenrick could set up anything for us, and I was sure he had done his research. We could always depend on Kenrick to completely and thoroughly accomplish any task he was set on doing. We were in good hands and we were about to have a great secret adventure.

We kept on walking, and I was really getting excited. I felt like jumping up and down, skipping down the path, but I couldn't get ahead of the others because I didn't know where we were going. I didn't know how they could contain their enthusiasm, unless going on a secret adventure was just an every day occurrence with them. I kept my eyes peeled to see where we might be going, but I didn't see anything ahead of us, or in any direction, for that matter.

"Yes!" Big Hawk shouted. "I knew it!"

"Knew what?" I asked. I looked around to see what he might have discovered, but all I could see were the path, the plains and the low bushes.

"We are going to the airport!" he said enthusiastically. His grin was contagious.

"We are going to the airport?" I asked. This could be really fun – and really dangerous.

"Yes, we are," Kenrick confirmed, nodding slightly.

"How do you know we're going to the airport?" I asked, scanning the landscape.

"It's right up there," Big Hawk said. Well, he was more than a foot taller than I was, but how could he see that much farther than I could?

"Where?" I asked, trying to make myself taller by standing on my toes and stretching my neck. I didn't see anything ahead of us, beside us, or in any direction. Shouldn't we be able to see some planes or helicopters or space ships or something, maybe a control tower?

"It's right up there," Kenrick said, pointing.

I still didn't see anything. Hiding Cathy began to laugh.

"Why is it funny?" I asked, searching for something that would indicate an airport was ahead of us.

"Just keep looking," Big Hawk said.

I was looking! And I wasn't seeing anything! "Where?"

My three friends were all laughing and looking,

apparently seeing something I couldn't see.

"Do I need special glasses or something?" I asked. I had had lens implants years ago to correct my vision, but my corrected eyes still couldn't see an airport in front of us. All I could see was the plain plain! Hmmm, that was interesting, there were no bushes in the area.

"Look at the path," Kenrick said, "under our feet."

I looked and I noticed the ground had become very firm. I looked ahead of us and my eyes tried to play tricks on me. I blinked and I could almost see something. I blinked again and that something was gone. I blinked twice, hard, and I could see something. Several airplanes were sitting in an area ahead of us, but they were really hard to see. Then I couldn't see them; then they reappeared again.

"The cammy paint," Big Hawk said. "It's so cool, so fantastic, just another wonder of our technology. I worked on this project last year, but this is the first time I got to see it on planes."

"What are you talking about?" I asked, trying to see the plane that had disappeared again. This was not a department where I worked or had heard of – but it was extremely interesting to see it in use.

"Camouflage paint," Hiding Cathy said. "These planes are fantastic. They are so hard to see, on the ground or in the air, but they are just like normal, anti-radar detectable planes. They can fly anywhere, they can land on any flat surface, and they are fast and comfortable. Have you ever been on a plane, Layla?"

"I'm sure I have but I don't remember," I said. I must have been transported by plane from our former home to this place; one of the old planes, in the old days, before The Great Devastation. I just had a gap in my memory, the part that got me from there to here. It was as if I went to sleep there and I woke up here, but time had passed and people were gone out of my life. My life had taken a completely different direction; well, all life had taken a new direction. We had to do things differently, since there weren't a lot of people left, and so many things and places had been destroyed. Even our State was merely a portion of the great country it had been, after the floods and earthquakes and fires caused by all the bombings, and most of the smaller countries no longer existed. Many of the former land masses were under water now.

We still had a distance to walk before we would be approaching the planes. At first it seemed odd that there was no fence around the area; then I thought, why would they fence it? Only people who had clearance could walk here from the Complex, and, from what Hiding Cathy had told me, none of the Outsider Communities were anywhere near here. An Outsider would have to walk for days and days to get here, through many areas covered with monitor cameras, and even if they somehow made it to this place, they couldn't fly or even board a plane without clearance. I was again amazed at what Kenrick was able to accomplish – but then, if he couldn't do it, nobody could. He was the one who had programmed the plane devices in the first place.

"So, we're flying someplace?" Hiding Cathy asked.

"Indeed we are," Big Hawk answered, giving us a big grin that showed all of his teeth.

"Can we go somewhere warm?" she asked. "Like, really warm?"

"We will go to a warm place," Kenrick said, nodding. I figured he had already planned the entire travel arrangements; he wasn't taking suggestions from us.

"But not too hot," Big Hawk said. "I don't like to get too hot."

"I wouldn't worry about it this time of the year," I said, "unless we are going to the southern hemisphere, where it is really hot."

"It won't be too hot where we're going, I promise," Kenrick said. "But we will be going to a warm place."

"So, where are we going?" I asked him again, not really expecting him to tell us yet.

"Just relax, we'll all enjoy ourselves," Kenrick promised.

We were approaching one of the planes, and now that we were so close to it, I could really see it. It didn't disappear and reappear like it had been doing when we were farther away from it. It was enormous, and it was beautiful. Close up, it kind of had a watery look, as if it were made of a translucent liquid.

"Quick!" Hiding Cathy said quietly, motioning for us to follow her. We stepped kind of sideways and before I knew it, we were in a small shelter, a shed of some sort that was hidden in the landscape. Hiding Cathy slithered out from among us and effortlessly closed the door. Obviously, she had done this before. She had known this invisible shack was here. She had probably flown all over the place. I never really thought about where she went on her missions. That she might have been going to places by invisible plane hadn't even entered my mind.

We stayed where we were, frozen in place. My heart again was pounding. I strained my ears to hear what was happening outside the shed. It sounded like movement of people, stepping, walking, stuff being shuffled from place to place.

"Oh, it's you," I heard a male voice say.

"Marco," Hiding Cathy said. Who was Marco? "Where's Polo?"

"We just got back but he has another assignment," Marco said. "Are you going or coming? Who are you with?" I could imagine he was looking around for her traveling companions.

"I just got back, too," she said. "Let's walk back together."

"I need to put my supplies away," Marco said.

"Here, give them to me, I'm putting my backpack away, too," Hiding Cathy said quickly. Suddenly she was at the door, her white-blond hair flashing in the sunlight as the door opened and she was in, moving and putting things in the corner, and out of the shed in record time. She just gave us a brief signal to go on with our travel. She was saving our reputations and jobs, and possibly our lives, and she was sacrificing her own chance to go with us. I tried to reason that she often traveled, and that it was no big deal to her; but traveling for work could not be nearly as fun as traveling with friends, especially with friends on a secret adventure to a surprise location.

We listened for them to leave and waited for at least ten minutes after we thought they were out of range before we opened the door. Who else might be outside that could catch us in the act of escaping? We dared not speak to each other or move a muscle until we were sure nobody else was in the area.

As Kenrick reached to open the door, a thought occurred to me. "What about this Polo person?" I whispered. "That Marco guy said he has another assignment. He could be somewhere around here."

"Don't worry about him," Kenrick said confidently.

"You know him?" Big Hawk asked.

"I know of him," Kenrick said. He stuck his head out of the door, slowly. "All clear, let's go. To that plane. Right there. Move fast."

We scampered across the compact ground to the plane and a door opened, letting down a staircase. Kenrick climbed up first, I followed him, and Big Hawk was right behind me. As soon as we were inside the plane, the door closed.

The interior of the plane was gorgeous. A deep velvet red covered the walls and the seats. A number of windows were all around the cabin, windows that couldn't be seen from the outside, I noted. The place was so plush and so comfortable-looking, so inviting, I moved right into place. The seat I selected wrapped around me as if it were my own.

A thought occurred to me. "Where's the pilot?" I asked.

"Right here!" Big Hawk said with a huge smile. He had to be kidding.

"You?" I asked. "You haven't flown a plane. I know you haven't." This could be scary.

"Well, not exactly," he said, "but I have clocked more than 1000 simulator hours."

"That's not flying experience!" I said, trying not to panic.

"I've made level Q, the highest level," he said.

"Yeah, the highest level on the ground," I said, hoping this was a joke.

"I also have more than 1000 simulator hours," Kenrick said, moving toward the cockpit. That didn't help my confidence level much.

"Flying a real plane with real people inside is not like flying a simulator!" I said.

"Have you ever flown a simulator?" Big Hawk asked.

"No, I–" I began.

"All you do is puzzles and games," Big Hawk said, "not real-life trainings."

"A simulator is like a game!" I said. "How many times have you crashed?"

"I haven't crashed at all while flying," Big Hawk said.

"Neither have I," Kenrick said.

"What about while landing?" I asked.

"At first, I was only three out of four, but now I never crash land any more," Big Hawk said. Now, THAT was reassuring!

"Neither do I," Kenrick said.

I didn't like it. I was scared. I didn't like to take any risks, well, any beyond what we were already taking by even being here. I hadn't thought about this type of safety! Was it too late for me to turn back now?

"You need to stash your stuff, take your seats, buckle up, and we are taking off in just a moment," a man in the cockpit said in one breath, peeking his head around the side of the door, and scaring me about half out of my mind. He was a handsome man, with black hair and clear blue eyes, and he was wearing a uniform – a pilot's uniform.

"Polo," Kenrick said, sitting in one of the pilot seats. "Don't we have a few minutes before take-off?" he asked.

"Not with the Patrol out there," Polo said, as he returned to his seat in the cockpit.

The Patrol were out there? As I was quickly buckling my seat belt, I looked out a window and I saw a line of armed men quickly approaching the plane. I knew the plane was bullet proof, everyone knew that all planes were, but I was scared. Who were they? Where did they get those guns? Why were they here? What did they want? We were so close to escaping, and we were going to get caught!

CHAPTER 5

The plane began to move with a jerk, and I saw several of the men fall to the ground to avoid being hit by the wing. I could see their mouths moving and I could imagine what they might be saying, but once the plane started, they couldn't stop it. They couldn't even see it, really, and they didn't know who was inside it: they didn't know WE were inside it. We could see them and they couldn't see us.

The plane moved down the camouflaged runway and I felt my heart leap to my throat as it left the ground. The Patrol were left behind, unable to catch us or track where we were going. I was so relieved that we had a real pilot and we weren't going to depend solely upon my two pilot-simulator friends. I had no problem with Kenrick assisting the pilot, or even flying the plane with the pilot beside him, as long as we had a real pilot who had real flying experience. I assumed Polo was a real pilot. I didn't want to question it now. He was wearing the uniform. He had done an excellent job taking off, and now that we were in the air and the land below us was shrinking, everything seemed to be fine. I relaxed a little.

Once we were at a level flying altitude, Kenrick came out of the cockpit and sat down with us in a comfy chair.

"This is the plane the Dignitaries use," he said.

"Good job!" Big Hawk said. "You really set us up! So, where are all the goodies?" He got out of his seat and began pressing against the walls of the cabin.

"Goodies?" I asked. "What do you mean?" I didn't realize until that moment that I was so ignorant! Why did they know all these things that I didn't know?

"They keep all their goodies, the neat little things they use when they travel, on the plane," Big Hawk explained, looking for possible hiding places.

"Like what?" I asked. The cabin itself was the most comfortable room I had ever seen – what other kinds of 'goodies' could they possibly want?

"Like this!" Kenrick said. He pressed a button on his seat's hand rest and leaped out of his seat as one of the walls dissolved, revealing another section on the plane, behind the main cabin area. Inside this secret compartment were all kinds of foods, clothing, entertainment devices and places to relax. It was like the inside of one of those mansions of Life Before I had read about, with every convenience and comfort a person could desire. At the Complex, we had every need satisfied, but this was just fantastic, beyond simple satisfaction.

"Whoa," Big Hawk said, clearly astonished. He began examining the goodies.

"When the Dignitaries go visit other areas, they use this as their base; a hotel that goes with them where ever they go," Kenrick said.

"I had no idea," I said. It's not that I had no imagination; I had just never thought about anything like this before. I did have, somewhere very deep, a memory of a plane: rows of seats filled with people, and that was it. In my mind, the inside of a plane was rows of seats. Well, in my mind, the outside of a plane was visible for all to see. This, obviously, was not an ordinary plane. Or was it? Maybe this was the only type of plane that existed any more.

"Just to let you know, this plane has cameras, inside and out, but I disabled all of them, along with the listening devices," Kenrick said.

"Oh, man, you watched them before, didn't you?" Big Hawk said. "On the plane, when they were going places? You spied on them."

"Let's just say I had a hand in some of the programming," Kenrick said with a smile. That statement told me that he was able to watch everything that transpired in this plane, probably from his home, or even on his Wat-Com. He probably listened to their conversations, too. As a matter of fact, Kenrick was probably the one who had done all the programming. He was the smartest person at the Complex when it came to computers and technology. He knew everything about them.

"So, what do you want?" Kenrick asked.

"I am a little hungry," I said, walking over to take a closer look at the variety of available food.

"Ken-man, you're sure no one else can see us while we're here?" Big Hawk asked. "Where are the cameras, anyway?"

Kenrick pointed to several pin holes in a metal rim that went around the cabin. "Camera, there, there, there, there, there, and there. And don't worry, no one can see anything unless they have my password, which is 42 random letters, numbers and symbols that I have not recorded anywhere back at the Complex."

"Is it in your Wat-Com?" Big Hawk asked, opening an enormous cooler, revealing a plethora of chilled foods and drinks.

"It's in my head, and no where else," Kenrick assured him, tapping the side of his head with his index finger.

"Hey, they have Kenny Sandwiches. You guys want

one?" Big Hawk asked.

A Kenny Sandwich was a type of sandwich Kenrick had suggested, and they had named it after him. It was made of avocados, tomatoes, sprouts and soy cheese on whole wheat bread. I loved them. I ate one at least once a week. In fact, that sounded good right now.

"Sure, I'll have one," I said, then I thought of something. "Won't they notice if things are missing?"

"I already have it scheduled to be restocked," Kenrick said. Why had I doubted him? Kenrick, as usual, had thought of everything.

Big Hawk handed me a sandwich, which was sealed in a reusable container.

"Thanks," I said.

"Want some juice to go with it?" he asked.

"How about some soy milk?" I said.

"One soy milk, coming right up!" Big Hawk said. He tossed me a single-serving container of soy milk, which I caught with both hands. He was really enjoying this. Well, we all were. I felt bad about Hiding Cathy not being able to come with us, though.

"What about Hiding Cathy?" I asked. "Won't she get in trouble for being there when she's scheduled to be gone?"

"I have already taken care of it," Kenrick said, browsing the selection of food.

"Of course you have!" Big Hawk said confidently.

"Of course you have," I repeated, wondering why I even questioned.

I went into the washroom, where the walls were lined with blue velvet. Some heavenly scent was hanging in the air. I inhaled deeply and felt completely relaxed. I washed my hands and prepared to eat.

Big Hawk was helping himself to all kinds of food. He was a big eater. He was a big person, so he could eat a lot. After he and Kenrick had selected their food and drinks, we sat down at a round table to eat. The food was really good, somehow even better tasting than the food we usually ate. Maybe it tasted better because of the excitement of the travel. Or, maybe it really was better.

"You know one thing I miss?" Big Hawk said, with his mouth full.

"The requirement to follow the rules of manners?" I asked.

"Yeah," he began, nodding and chewing, then he corrected himself. "No! No, I mean from Life Before, what I really miss."

"Your family?" I asked. "Love? Freedom? Music that wasn't selected and filtered by some old people?"

"Free television?" Kenrick asked. He was going way back.

"Well, yeah," Big Hawk said, "of course I miss all that. But what I really miss are the holidays we had."

"You mean Mandatory Days Off?" Kenrick asked, grabbing a handful of almonds. "We get lots of those." He tossed the almonds into his mouth, one at a time.

Holidays… a memory was triggered in my mind. An old feeling came over me, a feeling from my Life Before. We had celebrated holidays. I wondered if Kenrick was too young to remember family holidays or if his family hadn't celebrated holidays.

"Holidays were not like Mandatory Days Off," I

said, shaking my head, thinking of my family, almost remembering.

"Not at all!" Big Hawk said, taking a drink from a juice bottle. "They were family celebration times. Our family always had a big gathering for Easter."

"Easter?" Kenrick said. "Yeah, I read about that. People worshipped a bunny rabbit and ate a lot of chocolate eggs. I don't think my family ever celebrated the bunny day."

"No," Big Hawk said calmly as he leaned back in his chair. I knew we were going to get a nice, long story, told in his drawn out cadence. "Easter wasn't a celebration of a bunny day. Easter was a celebration of the most important event that has ever happened – the day Jesus Christ rose from the dead."

"You actually believe that old fable?" Kenrick asked.

"It's not a fable," I protested. That was something I did remember, something I had never forgotten. "It's the truth. No matter what the State has told us, and no matter what they want us to believe or not believe, it's still true. Jesus Christ is the Son of God, and on the third day after He was crucified, He rose from the dead, proving that He is the Son of God and that He has power over death. And that third day, the day He rose, we celebrated as Easter."

"Thank you, Layla, for that history lesson," Big Hawk said. He sat up straight, leaning his elbows on the table. "So, my family celebrated Easter as the most important holiday of the year. We never could get the whole family together for Christmas, because of schedules and the weather. We lived where there was a lot of snow in the winter, so we always had our big family gathering at Easter.

"All the family would decide on one house to visit each Easter. I loved to go to my Grandma's house and to my cousins' house, but I really loved it when the whole family came to my house."

"You had a large family?" Kenrick asked.

"My mom and dad each had two brothers and two sisters," Big Hawk said. "I had eight aunts and eight uncles, and 14 cousins. With me and my brother, that made 16 kids, so we really had lots of fun. Then there was my Grandma and Grandpa on my mom's side, and my Grandma and my great-grandma, Nana, on my Dad's side." He took a big gulp of his juice. "When all the families were coming to our house, my mom would start to get the house ready a week before Easter."

"What day was Easter on?" Kenrick said, sipping his drink through a straw. I was mildly surprised that he didn't know. I kind of thought he knew everything.

"It was on a Sunday in the spring," I recalled. "It wasn't on the same day every year."

"Yeah, it was on the first Sunday after the first full moon after the first day of spring," Big Hawk said. "By then, the snow was usually melted and roads were open for travel." He gobbled down some sesame stick snacks.

"Anyway, my mom would wash all the linens and my dad would get out the spare beds and the sleeping bags, and they would go shopping for the holiday food. That was one of the best parts, besides the cousins being at our house all weekend, all the good food we would have. They would get a ham and a turkey and my mom would bake a few cakes and at least four pies – have you ever had a home made pie?"

"Can't remember that I ever did," Kenrick said, as he took a bite of an organic energy bar. "Complex-made pie, yes."

"My mom used to make a nice apple pie," I said, remembering, "and my Aunt Moon would sometimes make chocolate pies. That was Before, when they didn't know how bad sugar was for us, and we could eat as much as we wanted." I had another memory flash: making frosting out of powdered sugar and milk and spreading it on cookies and graham crackers. We didn't have any of those items at the Complex.

"Yes! Apple pies!" Big Hawk said excitedly. "Hmm, I'm not sure about chocolate pies. But my mom would make apple pies and peach pies and banana cream pies and rhubarb pies and walnut pies."

"What's a rhubarb?" Kenrick asked, opening a package of organic raisins.

"Some kind of fruit," Big Hawk said. "Look it up when we get back to the Complex."

"I will," Kenrick promised. "You can be sure of that. If I had on my Water Closet, I'd look it up now."

"Go on with your story," I said to Big Hawk. It was nice to hear and think about families.

"Well, our house wasn't that big, but we had a couple of rooms in the attic where we kids would get to sleep, all of us, and our grandparents and aunts and uncles would sleep in our bedrooms and the guest room, and on the couches downstairs. We would make our blankets into tents and tell funny and scary stories to each other. We would stay up just about the whole night talking on Friday night. We would go out and play all day on Saturday, down to the creek if it was thawed, or we would just play in the fields. We had eight boys and eight girls, so we would sometimes play games and have teams. We would play, oh, you know, maybe soccer or badminton or volleyball. Or sometimes we would just play tag, or hide and seek."

"Wow, I don't remember playing any of those games," I said, bringing back a portion of my Life Before. "I did a lot of swimming and skating, mostly with my dad, but I didn't have any brothers or sisters, and the only family I knew besides my parents were my Aunt Moon and Uncle Pierce. I didn't really play a lot with the other kids."

"Me, neither," Kenrick said. "I was an only child, and my parents spent all of their time on the computers, so, I did, too. We had 12 computers at our house." He smiled nostalgically.

"So," Big Hawk continued, "we would have a blast on Saturday, and then we would get cleaned up so we could go to Sunrise Service at church on Easter Sunday. My family went to church every Sunday. It was a small church, and when my whole family was there for Easter Sunday, we would more than double the size of the congregation.

"We would all get up really early on Sunday morning and put on our best clothes, and we would all walk to church in the dark, before the sun came up. It wasn't very far from the house, about a ten minute walk. So, all of us, 16 kids and 22 adults, even Nana, would walk to church. Then we would celebrate the rising of Jesus as the sun was rising. We would sing all the Easter songs – I wish I could remember just one now – and we would listen to the preacher talk about Jesus, when He was crucified, nailed to the cross on Friday and how He rose from the dead on Easter Sunday."

"He was nailed to a cross, and you celebrated that?" Kenrick said, making a face. "I don't get it."

"Well, He died for the sins of the world," Big Hawk said.

"Sins?" Kenrick asked. "What are sins?"

"Something no one at the Complex will ever admit," I said.

"Yeah, they justify everything they do," Big Hawk said. "Whenever they want to justify a sin, they just change a law or a rule so their sins are accepted, so they are not sins."

"So, what's a sin?" Kenrick asked.

"A sin is something that is contrary to the laws of God," Big Hawk said.

"But we don't observe those old laws anymore," Kenrick said.

"Yeah, that's what I'm saying," Big Hawk said. "Our society has changed all the rules, so, whatever they say is right is right."

"What's wrong with that?" Kenrick said. "It's what is accepted by the leaders, and, therefore, the followers; the Insiders and the Outsiders."

"But that doesn't make it right," I said, feeling an awakening of my moral roots. We had been brainwashed for so long, I had almost begun to ignore my conscience. I was glad Big Hawk was reviving my old inner self.

"It has been decided that there is no God," Kenrick said. "You guys know that. We can't talk about Him. We can't worship Him. He doesn't exist."

"Just saying that He doesn't exist doesn't mean He doesn't exist," I said. "I KNOW He exists."

"How do you know?" Kenrick said. "You don't have any proof."

"I can feel Him, inside my heart, inside my soul," I said.

"But it was agreed that He can't possibly exist. If He did exist, He never would have allowed The Great Devastation."

"That wasn't God's fault!" Big Hawk shouted, slapping the table. "It was because of the sinfulness of the people, and their rejection of Him!"

"Okay, take it easy," Kenrick said, holding up his hands in resignation. "Let's not make this into an argument. I don't care, you guys can believe anything you want to believe, but just don't let them know about it."

"Big Hawk, finish telling about your Easter celebrations," I said. He had such wonderful memories he was sharing, I didn't want to ruin the mood with a disagreement. It wasn't Kenrick's fault his parents never introduced him to Jesus.

Big Hawk proceeded. "So, after church, we would walk back home, and my mom and my aunts would get Easter dinner ready for us. I can just about smell it now. They spent all day Saturday cooking, so the food was ready for us when we got home, it just needed to be heated up and set on all the tables. My dad and my uncles would get the spare tables out of the garage, and they would set them up all over the place: in the kitchen, the dining room, the living room, on the front porch, which was enclosed, and on the back patio, if it was warm enough. When it was too cold to sit on the patio, some of us would end up eating in the basement, which was nice, because we had a wood stove down there, and it made the house nice and warm."

"Whoa! A wood stove?" I exclaimed. "You actually

burned wood?"

"Yeah, my dad and my uncles were always chopping wood for the stove."

"Where did they get the wood?" I asked. "I mean, did they get it from broken down buildings or something?"

"No, they got it from the forest."

"They just wasted trees like that?" I couldn't believe it. I couldn't remember many trees in Life Before, just a few small, scrawny ones, and they had been roped off, protected, so no one would accidentally bump or destroy them.

"No, there were plenty of trees all around our house," Big Hawk said, something I couldn't imagine. "Sometimes I went with my dad to get wood, in the forest, just behind our back yard. There were lots of trees there. We would find one that had fallen and chop it up into pieces that we could burn in the stove. We didn't cut down the living trees for wood."

"Whew!" I said, relaxing a bit. "That's a relief!"

"So, the whole family would all sit down for Easter dinner, usually at about one o'clock in the afternoon. Our parents and grandparents and aunts and uncles would be sitting in the dining room and living room, and we kids would fight over the other tables. We all tried to get the table in the kitchen, because whoever was in there when they served the pies got to pick first, but really, there was so much food, we never had a shortage." He had a pleasant look on his face, a half smile, as he relayed his memories to us.

"We would all eat so much food that we thought we would burst, then we would all go into the family room and sing," he continued. "Our family was like a choir, and we would sing all kinds of songs about Jesus. Then we would catch up on everything, you know, what we were doing in school, what sports we were learning, and we would all have time to talk to our grandparents and all our aunts and uncles before they got ready to leave. Usually my grandparents would come a few days early, and stay about a week, but the cousins could only stay the weekend because of school. We would promise to write to each other and we would say goodbye. Hugging everyone took about an hour. Sometimes during the year we would call or video conference or face-time each other, but nothing was like when we all got together at Easter."

"Did you try to find any of your family after The Great Devastation?" I asked, then I realized that was a useless question. Who hadn't tried to find their family members?

"Kenny and I searched the database, but we couldn't find any of their names among the living."

"I'm sorry," I said, my heart feeling heavy. His loss seemed so much greater than mine – I had only lost four people I loved, and that really hurt. He had lost 37 family members!

"So, where did the bunny come in?" Kenrick asked, seemingly unimpressed by Big Hawk's sentimental story. "And the chocolate eggs?"

"I'm not sure how that all came about," Big Hawk said, "but my grandmother said it was the way society had of distracting from the greatest thing God had done, raising Jesus from the dead."

"My dad said the same thing!" I recalled. My dad was so smart.

"So, Kenny, you didn't celebrate ANY holidays?"

Big Hawk asked.

"Nope," Kenrick confirmed, shaking his head.

"What about you, Layla?" Big Hawk asked. "Do you remember any holidays?"

"Yes, as a matter of fact, I do," I said, as the memories started to flow. I could begin to see it in my mind's eye as if I were reviewing a video. "I remember what they called the winter holidays, Thanksgiving and Christmas. Actually, our holidays started with Thanksgiving. We would get a big turkey–"

"Thanksgiving?" Kenrick asked. "I don't remember it, but I do remember Santa Claus. He was kind of scary to me, all big and fat and with that big beard and those beady eyes. I'm glad my parents didn't make me go see him."

"Okay, so, it's my turn," I said, not wanting to lose hold of my memories that were unfolding.

"Go ahead," Kenrick said, prompting me with his hands.

"Like I said, or I was starting to say, our holidays started with Thanksgiving. My mom would put a turkey in the oven early in the morning, and she would cook all day, all kinds of good things, and the house would be smelling good the whole day. My Aunt Moon and Uncle Pierce would come over to our house and Aunt Moon would help with the cooking. My mom always made the Thanksgiving dinner at our house, because Uncle Pierce was a pilot and sometimes he would be gone on Thanksgiving. So, we always had the dinner at our house. Our Thanksgiving dinner was turkey with corn bread-and-bacon stuffing, mashed potatoes and gravy, sweet potatoes, green bean casserole, dinner rolls and cranberry sauce. We ate dinner in the early afternoon on Thanksgiving Day. Before we started eating, we would go around the table and share what we were thankful for, and sometimes that would take a really long time, because we were so thankful for a lot of things in our lives. Then we would have pumpkin pie or apple pie for dessert. We had our dessert much later in the evening, because we were so full from the wonderful dinner."

Big Hawk was smiling. Kenrick looked a little bit bored with my story.

"So, that was the start of our holiday season. The day after Thanksgiving we would start listening to Christmas music – you know, that's one thing I really miss, the Christmas music. Sometimes I still sing it in my head. I know we're not allowed to listen to it or sing it at the Complex, but they have no control over what goes on in my head."

"Yes, they do," Kenrick said. "You would be surprised if you knew how much control they have over what goes on in our heads." He wiggled his fingers at me, like he was casting a spell.

"You mean, like programming us and stuff?" I asked.

Kenrick didn't answer. He just pursed his lips.

"So, you are an inner rebel, like me?" Big Hawk asked, turning to me.

"You're an inner rebel?" Kenrick asked Big Hawk. "I thought you were flat-out defiant."

"Not exactly," Big Hawk said mischievously. "So, Layla, what's your favorite Christmas song?"

I still remembered some Christmas songs. "I used to love 'Joy to the World,' but after I lost my family, I had a hard time feeling that joy, so I started to love 'O Come, All Ye Faithful,' because it says, 'all ye citizens of heaven,' and that is what we are. My family is there now, and I'll be there with them some day. That's really comforting to me. And I also loved it when my mom and my Aunt Moon sang 'Angels We Have Heard On High.' That was a really pretty song and they harmonized beautifully, like only sisters can. Their voices just blended."

"My favorite Christmas song has always been 'Silent Night,' because I can just imagine a quiet and holy night when Jesus was born," Big Hawk said. "I also really like 'Hark! The Herald Angels Sing,' because I could just imagine being one of those shepherds out in the field when the angels came to them and told them the Son of God had just been born. Can you picture it, first one angel and the glory of the Lord lighting up the sky, and then the whole sky filled with angels, singing, 'glory to God in the highest, and on earth, peace, good will toward men!' It must have been a truly glorious sight."

"And you really believe that?" Kenrick asked, snorting.

"With all my heart and all my mind," Big Hawk stated.

"Me, too," I said.

"Interesting. I thought you two were more logical than that," Kenrick said.

"Oh, once you get to know God, it's more than logical," Big Hawk said.

"His Way is the only thing that could possibly be logical," I added.

"Okay, you guys can have your beliefs, but it's a good thing you keep them secret, because they will label you as crazy and put you away," Kenrick warned. "You will no doubt be put out of the Complex if they hear any talk like this."

Big Hawk and I were already aware of that. They had done what they could to squash our beliefs, but they hadn't been able to take them from us. I was feeling strengthened by Big Hawk's bold admissions, and I didn't want to hide my love of Jesus any more. I remembered, before The Great Devastation, when we had been free to admit we were Christians. However, I didn't even know if there were any other Believers at the Complex. No one would – or could – ever admit it.

"So, Layla," Big Hawk said, settling into his chair, "finish your story about your holidays."

"Oh, yeah," I said, letting the memories fill my mind, "the Christmas music… we would start listening to it the day after Thanksgiving. My mom had a rule: we couldn't listen to any Christmas music before Thanksgiving, but on the day after, we would start listening to it. That weekend after Thanksgiving – oh, do you remember? Thanksgiving was always celebrated on the fourth Thursday of November, so it was just about a month between Thanksgiving and Christmas, and the whole season for us would be a time of celebration."

Big Hawk nodded in agreement. Kenrick was looking at me as if I were muttering gibberish.

"On the weekend after Thanksgiving, my mom would do all the Christmas cards," I said. "Do you guys remember that tradition?"

"Yeah, my mom would do the same thing," Big Hawk said, nodding his head. "She would send out a bunch of cards with pictures of our family to all our friends and family, and we would receive cards from everyone we knew, with pictures and poems and notes of encouragement. It was so fun to hear from everyone."

"We didn't do that," Kenrick said. He sounded kind of disappointed. "As a matter of fact, we didn't have anything to do with the physical mail. We sent and received everything electronically."

"Yeah, everything was going in that direction, but my mom always loved to do the Christmas cards," I said. "I liked them, too," I admitted.

"Me, too," Big Hawk agreed. "My mom would put them up all over the wall and we could look at them for a couple of months, until she finally decided to take them down. She put them in a box, to save them forever, I guess. Who knows what ever happened to them?"

"They are probably still in your house, if it's still standing," Kenrick said.

"I'll never know," Big Hawk said, with a note of sadness. "I'm never going back there again."

"Never say never," Kenrick said, "because you never know."

I didn't try to figure out what he meant... but, could we be going there? Or was he making a play on words?

"So, anyway, back to our holidays," I said, looking up in the corner of the cabin to help me remember. "My dad and Uncle Pierce put up strings of colored lights, blinking lights, all outside both of our houses, ours and theirs, right after Thanksgiving. Every year they would buy more, so we would have more and more Christmas lights on at night, and then everyone in the neighborhood started putting up lights too, so the whole place was lit up like some kind of fantasy land every night during the Christmas season." I smiled at the happy memory.

"Oh, yeah, we had an artificial Christmas tree that was fashioned to look just like the real thing. We had one and my aunt and uncle had one, and we would put them up in our houses in the beginning of December."

"Wait!" Kenrick said. "You took a tree inside your house? A real tree? Now that is just weird."

"It wasn't a real tree, it was an artificial one, but it was made to look like a real tree, and we decorated it with all kinds of Christmas decorations."

"What's a Christmas decoration?" Kenrick asked, shaking his head. "What do you mean by that?"

"We always had a real Christmas tree," Big Hawk said, ignoring Kenrick's question.

"You had a real, live Christmas tree?" I asked. "But wasn't that a waste of a tree, just to cut it down and take it in the house for a few weeks? So, you must have used a different one every year!" I was really missing trees. I couldn't imagine using a tree like that, especially since I had never lived near any amount of trees.

"There were so many trees in the woods near us, and my dad would find one that needed to be cut down," Big Hawk said.

"No tree ever needed to be cut down!" I protested.

"In the forest, back then, the trees would grow really dense," Big Hawk said, "and there were some that were not growing well because the trees were too close together. They had to be thinned out."

I still couldn't imagine it. After The Great Devastation, there were only a few trees left on the earth, and I could remember seeing only one, the one I had hugged today.

"I still don't get it," Kenrick said. "Why did you

take a tree, living or a fake one, inside your house? Didn't the leaves fall off all over the floor and make a huge mess?" He shuddered, appalled.

"A Christmas tree was an evergreen tree," Big Hawk said. "Evergreens had needles, not leaves, and they didn't lose them in the winter."

I didn't know if any evergreen trees still existed.

"You're not serious," Kenrick said. He looked at us as if we were just joshing with him.

"It was a tradition," I said, the only explanation I could think of. I really didn't know why we did it, or what it represented.

"Yeah, the Christmas tree tradition," Big Hawk said. "Everyone we knew did that."

"I never saw a house with a tree inside it," Kenrick said. "I don't get it. As a matter of fact, I can't remember seeing a house with a tree outside of it."

I felt kind of sorry for him. He really didn't know what he had been missing.

"So, we decorated our Christmas tree with lights and shiny bells and balls and we would hang special ornaments on it, and make it look really pretty," I said.

"That seems bizarre," Kenrick said. "A decorated tree. I would say that was a waste of time, effort and money. What did you do with it? Or, what did it do?"

"We just looked at it," I said, not really knowing what we had done with it.

"It was really enjoyable," Big Hawk said.

"I guess you had to be there," Kenrick said.

"We would save the ornaments and use them every year," I said. "We would make some ornaments, and some we would get as gifts, and some we would buy. Every year we would try to make our tree look prettier than the last year."

"Yeah, we did that, and also we would string popcorn and put it on the trees outside our house for the birds," Big Hawk said.

"You had trees in your yard, too?" I tried not to let my jealousy show.

"Yeah, we had them all around the house, oh, probably about fifteen trees were in our yard," he said. "They really protected the house from the sun in the summer. My mom always said the house was 20 degrees cooler because of the shade from the trees."

"That's pretty cool," Kenrick stated. I didn't know if he was making sport of Big Hawk or making a play on words, but I agreed that it was very cool. I still would have been fascinated by trees if we had them all over the place. It wasn't just because we didn't have them that I loved them.

"So, you decorated a tree inside your house, and then what?" Kenrick said.

"We decorated the whole house," I said. "We had special red and green towels and table cloths and we had all kinds of decorations, like candles and fancy wreaths. We had a little manger scene we set up on the living room table."

"You had one of those?" Big Hawk said. "We did, too. My mom really loved it."

"What's a manger scene?" Kenrick said.

"Well, it represented the real meaning of Christmas," I said.

"The real meaning of Christmas?" Kenrick asked. "I

don't even know the fake meaning of Christmas. What's the real meaning of Christmas?"

"I got this," Big Hawk said, nodding to me. I could see he was going into a preacher mode, so I let him take it. "We celebrated Christmas as the day Jesus Christ was born in a manger."

"Jesus, again? What's a manger?" Kenrick said.

This was going to take a lot of explanation.

"It's like a trough that animals ate out of, like horses and cows," Big Hawk answered.

"I don't get it," Kenrick asked, clearly confused. "Why would any one be born in a manger?"

"Because there was no room at the inn," I said.

"Huh?" Kenrick asked. "What inn?"

Big Hawk smiled, as if he were teaching a Sunday School class to children. "His parents, Mary and Joseph, were traveling. They had to return to Bethlehem, their family home, for the census, and his mother was pregnant," he said, "but Jesus is actually the Son of God, so Joseph wasn't his real father, and the Holy Ghost came upon Mary, who was a virgin. So, when Mary and Joseph went to Bethlehem, there were so many people there, because of the census, Mary and Joseph had to stay in a stable with the animals, and it was there that Jesus was born. Since they didn't have any other place for Him, they put Him in a manger."

"Wow, I never heard of anything like that," Kenrick said.

"There *is* nothing like it," Big Hawk agreed.

"I think it must have been kind of nice," I said, "for them to be there with all the animals instead of being inside some crowded rooming house with all those people and the noise. I like animals."

"When have you ever seen an animal," Kenrick snorted, "except on a monitor? Oh, and the cows we saw today."

"I remember animals," I said. "My parents, when I was young, took me to a zoo, and I saw all kinds of animals."

"You went to a zoo?" Kenrick asked incredulously. "Yeah, I read about those. I saw some videos and some animations of what kinds of animals must have lived in them."

"Well, we went to a real zoo and I saw them," I said. "They were real, live animals. I could see them up close. I saw elephants and tigers and elk and penguins and giraffes and mountain goats and zebras and monkeys and bears, all kinds of bears, and camels. The camels were really strange. They were a lot bigger than I thought they would be." I felt really sad when I thought about the thousands of species of animals that were annihilated during and after The Great Devastation, either due to the actual disasters or the destruction of their habitats.

"They just seemed big because you were so small," Kenrick said, laughing.

"No, I saw them, too," Big Hawk said, "at a zoo, too. The camels were really big, but the elephants were much, much bigger than the camels."

"Yeah, the elephants were much bigger than the camels," I agreed, nodding and remembering.

"So, I'm the only one of us who never had a chance to go to a zoo?" Kenrick said. "I had no idea what I was missing. They make it seem like it was no big deal."

"They do minimize the importance of everything in the past," Big Hawk said.

"So, what was so great about animals, if you didn't eat them?" Kenrick asked.

"We had pets that were part of our family," Big Hawk said.

"You had pets?" I asked. That would have been a dream come true! "What kind of pets did you have?"

"We had two dogs and four cats," Big Hawk said, "and my brother had fish."

"Fish?" Kenrick asked. "What kind of pets were fish? Did you play with them?"

"No, these were little fish, and we had a fish tank, and they would swim around in there and we would watch them."

"Oh, really, that sounds like some kind of fun," Kenrick said sarcastically.

I was impressed, even if Kenrick didn't seem to be. "You had dogs and cats? Did you let them come in your house?"

"Yeah, they were always in the house," Big Hawk said, "in and out, all the time. The dogs liked to follow us all around, whatever we were doing, and the cats kind of did their own thing, but they liked to be around us, too."

"Your parents let animals come in the house?" Kenrick asked. He looked disgusted.

"It was their idea," Big Hawk said, "because they had pets before my brother and I were even born."

"Did you have names for your pets?" I asked.

"Of course we did!" Big Hawk said. "They had to have names! They were members of our family. We had one dog named Miller, he was a yellowish color, a Golden Lab. Mishka was black and white, a Border Collie. Our cats were named Midnight, he was all black, and really sleek, and huge, with a very long body, and then we had Twinkle, she was Siamese with really long hair and she had pretty blue eyes, and then we had two ginger tabby cats, Patty and Jazzie. They were yellowish and orangish and white striped cats."

"What's a tabby cat?" Kenrick asked.

"A tabby cat had patterns of gray and black and white, or orange or red or yellow and had a distinctive coat of stripes, dots, or swirling patterns, and it usually had an 'M' mark on its forehead. Patty and Jazzie both had dark orange Ms. Sometimes a tabby cat had a white chest or white feet. Tabby cats were the friendliest kinds of cats, and they would talk to us the most."

"They could talk?" Kenrick said, his eyes widening. "What language did they speak?"

"Cat language," Big Hawk laughed. "They were meowing at us all the time, every time they saw us. And they loved to climb the Christmas tree!" he laughed. "They would be chasing each other around the house, especially when they were kittens, and they would climb the Christmas tree and knock it over, and all the ornaments would go flying around the room. Then we would rush into the room to see what happened, and they would sit there and look at us like it was our fault. It was like they were saying, 'we didn't do it!' "

"I bet your parents were really mad," Kenrick said. I could tell he didn't have a love of animals. Well, how could he, if he had never seen any?

"No, my parents loved cats," Big Hawk said. "They just laughed and made my brother and me clean up the mess and we had to put the tree back upright and then put all the decorations on it again."

"My mom and my Aunt Moon would always talk about the cats they had when they were growing up," I said. "You know, they had a cat named Patty, too, and I think it was an orange tabby, too."

"Patty is a perfect name for an orange tabby cat," Big Hawk said.

"It was," I said sadly. Even if there were any cats left on earth, we were not allowed to have any kind of animals at the Complex, not even fish in a tank. They were too afraid we would get diseases from them.

"Were they really soft, I mean, the fur?" I asked. I couldn't remember ever touching a cat, but I had seen a lot of pictures and animations of them.

"Yes, their fur was soft but their claws were sharp."

"They had claws?" Kenrick asked. Didn't he know anything about animals? He knew everything about computers. "Did they claw you? Did they hurt you?"

"You've been listening to too much Prop," Big Hawk said. "Sometimes our cats would scratch us, but it didn't really hurt, and it healed fast."

"Did they make you bleed?" Kenrick asked.

"Not enough to even mention," Big Hawk said. "The little bit of pain we got from them was worth the enormous amount of pleasure they gave us. You know, what they liked to do was open the Christmas presents. They would play with the ribbons and bows and tear off the wrapping paper."

"Christmas presents?" Kenrick asked. "What's a

Christmas present?"

"Yeah, I was getting to that part," I said. "Back to my holiday memories, guys. Where was I?"

"We were talking about Christmas trees and pets and animals," Kenrick said.

"Oh, yes," I said, "the manger scene. We would have a little manger scene with a little Mary and Joseph and baby Jesus in the manger, and all the animals in the stable around, along with the shepherds and the wise men who brought gifts to the newborn King."

"Which was Jesus," Big Hawk clarified.

"I'm going to have to do some research on this topic," Kenrick said. "It sounds kind of interesting."

"You'll never find anything about God or Christianity in the historical archives," Big Hawk said. "They wiped it all out, everything they could find. But, I do know where you can get a copy of the Bible. It tells you everything you need to know about God and His Son, Jesus."

"Including what we just told you," I added.

"I'll check into it," Kenrick told us.

"So, anyway," I continued, "in the weeks between Thanksgiving and Christmas, we would buy gifts for our family members and wrap them in fancy wrapping paper and put them under the Christmas tree."

"Waste of paper," Kenrick said. "You wrapped up gifts in paper and then after you took off the paper, what did you do with it?"

"We threw it away," Big Hawk said.

"I guess back then there were enough trees so we could waste paper that way," I said. "It seemed like there was wrapping paper all over the place. You could get it in any store."

"Sometimes we wrapped our gifts in newspaper," Big Hawk said.

"Newspaper?" Kenrick asked. "What's that?"

"During Life Before, every day, they printed the news on paper and they passed the papers out to everyone in town," Big Hawk said. "Well, everyone who paid for them, that is."

"Now, that was a waste of paper," Kenrick said. "We get all the news we need, more than we could ever read or watch or hear on the computer feeds and on our Water Closets."

"I can agree with that," I said, attempting to redirect the conversation. "So, getting back to our family celebration, we would get special gifts for everyone in the family. I would make gifts for everyone, and my dad especially liked all the gifts I made for him, like the time I knitted him a pair of slippers. They were lopsided and crooked, but he wore them and I could tell he loved them. Well, my mom loved my gifts, too, and Aunt Moon and Uncle Pierce did, too. They all liked the gifts I made, but I think it was just because I was a little kid and they liked everything I did. But my dad really let me know he thought the things I made for him were special."

"I'm sure they were," Kenrick said, giving me a patronizing smile.

"Another thing we did every year was make a gingerbread house," I said, recalling the fun process. That had been one of my favorite things to do. "My mom and my Aunt Moon and I would get all kinds of candy and we would bake the sides and the roof of the house out of gingerbread, like big cookies, shaped like walls and a roof, and then when they got cool, we would stick them together with frosting."

"Sugary frosting?" Kenrick asked. "You actually ate that? And you are still alive, all these years later, to tell us about it?"

"Yeah, I know," I said. "It would be impossible to get those ingredients today, but back then, they were in abundance. We could buy all kinds of bad foods that tasted good. We really had a lot of fun decorating the gingerbread houses. We decorated it with candy. We would use frosting to stick the candy all over the house in fancy patterns and make little windows and doors. We liked to make it look like the white icing was snow all over the roof. We would make it really pretty. Usually, Mom and Aunt Moon would make one really fancy house and they would let me decorate one of my own, however I wanted to make it. Then, after a couple of days, we would start to pick at the candy and eat the whole house, little by little. I would always make mine all sloppy with lots of frosting, so it was really much better to eat, much tastier. We never wanted to ruin the perfect gingerbread house that Mom and Aunt Moon made. We would take lots of pictures of it, and finally, after mine was all gone, about a week later, we would start to pick pieces from their house and eat it."

"That sounds like it was really fun," Big Hawk said. "I guess we didn't do that because we just had boys at home. But my mom did bake gingerbread every Christmas. It tasted much better than that stuff we get now at the Complex."

"But probably not better for you," Kenrick said quickly.

"Probably not," Big Hawk agreed. "But it tasted so good! So, Layla, what else did you do to celebrate, as you take us down memory lane of your holiday tradition?"

The memories were tumbling into my mind, one after another. "Well, something else we did, we went to see the Nutcracker ballet. A ballet troupe would come every Christmas season, and we always went to see it. One year, we even saw the Nutcracker on ice, where they skated to the music. Now, that is some music I would like to hear again some day. I wouldn't mind skating around the Complex to that music!"

"Okay, you lost me again," Kenrick said. "What on earth was the Nutcracker ballet?"

"You have heard of ballet dancing?" I asked.

"Yeah, some special kind of dancing where they did a lot of kicking and going up on their toes and they wore body suits," Big Hawk explained.

"You make it sound so... un-beautiful," I said. "It was one of the most beautiful and fascinating things I have ever seen. The Nutcracker was a story about a girl who had an eccentric uncle and her family had this great Christmas party and her uncle gave her this nutcracker doll and then she had a dream that he was a prince and she watched all of these beautiful dances from far away lands with him. Well, that's the Nutcracker in a nutshell."

"Well," Kenrick said, unimpressed.

"That's another thing we never did," Big Hawk said.

"Boys," I said. "Of course you wouldn't go to a ballet, and especially not the same ballet every year. Boys just wouldn't do that."

"Nope. We wouldn't," he agreed.

"I remember dancing," Kenrick said, an old memory suddenly kicking in. "My mother loved dancing. She didn't dance, but she loved to watch dancing on the monitors. She had her computer set to a dancing channel, so when she turned it on, she could watch a dance before she started work."

"Where did she work?" Big Hawk asked.

"She worked at home, on the computer," Kenrick said. "My dad did, too. I'm not sure what they were doing all the time, but they were working on something on their computers and sometimes I would help them. Or if my mom's computer broke down, she would have me fix it."

"That's funny," I said. "You knew how to fix your mom's computer and you were just a little kid, and she didn't know how to fix it."

"No, she knew how to fix it," Kenrick said. "She just taught me how to do it so I could fix it for her when it broke. She showed me how to run all the diagnostics, what were all the set-up patterns, how to check the system essentials and when to engage the virus zappers, and if the computer didn't respond at all, she taught me how to open it and check the circuits, and re-route them if I needed to, or change the central chips. I could always get it working for her."

"Did you ever think maybe she broke it on purpose, so you would have to learn to fix it?" Big Hawk said.

"No!" Kenrick shouted. "My mom would never do that!" He looked a little uncomfortable thinking about that possibility.

"We never really know why grown-ups do anything, or how they teach us things," Big Hawk said. "My dad would take my bike apart so I could put it back together."

"That was mean," I said.

"What do you mean?" Big Hawk asked.

"You wanted to ride your bike," I said, "and instead your dad took it all apart and you had to put it back together."

"I learned a lot from that," Big Hawk said.

"Yeah, I'm sure you did," Kenrick said. "Like, your dad didn't have enough to do keeping things together, so he had to take things apart."

"My dad took my bike apart a bunch of times, so I had a chance to learn how to put it back together," Big Hawk said. "Then, one time when my brother's bike broke down when we were on a long ride, I knew how to put it back together so we could ride home."

"Your dad was just messing with you," Kenrick said.

"Very funny," Big Hawk said defensively.

"Yeah, I forgot to laugh," I added, thinking about how awful that would have been, every time he wanted to go on a bike ride, he had to put his bike together again.

"So, that's it?" Kenrick said, turning to me. "The dancing ballet Nutcracker thing? That was the end of your family holiday?"

"No," I continued, "we had other traditions, too. We would go around the neighborhood and sing Christmas carols with a group of people from our church. And we would go sing at the hospital, to cheer up the sick people, and we would go caroling at the Homes, to cheer up the old people."

"Christmas carols?" Kenrick asked. "And they were...?"

"Christmas songs, the ones we would sing every

year at Christmas time, the ones about Jesus, and also enjoying the Christmas season, like 'Jingle Bells' and 'Deck the Halls' and songs like that."

"Never heard of them," Kenrick stated.

"You were too young and too sheltered," Big Hawk said. I nodded my head in agreement. "Go on, Layla, tell us the rest of your holiday traditions. I love to think back on those times."

"All month long, we would watch Christmas movies on the big screens, all about the miracles of Christmas–"

"Miracles!" Kenrick said. "We all know there is no such thing as miracles."

"No, we don't know that," Big Hawk said.

"I still believe in miracles," I said.

"I do, too," Big Hawk said. "We do not agree with the findings of the State on that. Miracles still happen, even today. Go on, Layla, if you can finish without Kenny interrupting you again."

"Okay, then, on December 24, which was Christmas Eve, the night before Christmas, we would go to a special service at church. There we would have a Christmas play or a Christmas program, and we would celebrate the birth of Christ together with our church family."

"You went to church?" Kenrick asked. "It was allowed in our lifetime?"

He must not have been paying attention when Big Hawk had just told us his family went to church on Easter.

"Yeah, in Life Before, they said people were healthier if they went to church and had a spiritual foundation," I said.

"It's true," Big Hawk said, nodding.

"It's obvious that being spiritual is better for people than not being spiritual," Kenrick said, "but what did that have to do with church?"

"Ahh, there are all kinds of spirits!" Big Hawk said. "You just have to have the right Spirit."

"The right Spirit?" Kenrick asked. For a Kidgen-Comgen, he sure didn't know anything about the spiritual realm. I had to admit, some of it I had forgotten, due to the squashing by the State, but it was deep down inside me, somewhere. I did know God and I did know who Jesus was, and I loved Him.

"The Holy Spirit," Big Hawk said. "That's the Spirit of God, that He sent down to indwell believers after Jesus ascended to heaven."

"I thought you said He rose from the grave," Kenrick said.

"He did," I said. "Then after He rose, He went to heaven, and He sent the Holy Spirit, the Spirit of God, to all the ones who believe in Him."

"Okay, that's over my head," Kenrick said, dismissing that conversation. "Give me a computer any day. Layla, go on with your story. It sounds so homey."

I gladly continued. It was fun remembering. "On December 25, the day we celebrated Christmas, we would get up early and we would all meet in the living room, the whole family. My Aunt Moon and Uncle Pierce would come over, and we would gather around the Christmas tree and open our presents.

"Then my dad would read the Christmas story about the birth of Jesus out of the Bible and we would all sing about Jesus and then we would pray together.

After that, Mom and Aunt Moon would make Christmas dinner. Sometimes it was the same as our Thanksgiving dinner, and sometimes we had ham instead of turkey, and we would have all the yummy things that went with it: the green beans, the sweet potatoes, the home-baked rolls, the pies. We would all eat a nice dinner and then we would relax together. My dad and Uncle Pierce would watch a football game on the big screen, and I would play with the new puzzles and games I got, and my mom and Aunt Moon would play cards or play games and talk and laugh a lot.

"We had a one week vacation and we would all relax together for that week. On New Year's Day, we would take down the Christmas tree and put away all the decorations and save them for the next year."

"Wow, that's really something." Kenrick said. "You remember all those details, still?"

"We did the same thing every year," I said, not wanting to admit that I had forgotten all about it until now, now that I was being urged to remember. The memories were so nice – but the reminder that they had ended was so painful. "It was our tradition." I leaned down to wipe a tear, so my friends wouldn't see it.

"Traditions were nice," Big Hawk said. "I miss traditions."

"Yeah, they don't want us to get too close to anything or to have any kind of sentiment," Kenrick said. "Then we might not do what they want us to do. We might want to do something on our own, without their permission or knowledge."

We all smiled at each other. Big Hawk burst out laughing. We were doing just that! The exact thing the State was trying so hard to prevent was happening right now! And we were doing it! We all knew, deep down, that in our hearts we were actually rebellious and we wanted to do things that were not allowed. We just had to appear to be perfectly compliant to all the rules while we were at the Complex.

"We had some Christmas traditions," Big Hawk said, "but we didn't always do exactly the same thing every year like your family did, Layla. Most of the time we would stay home for Christmas, and we had the Christmas tree and the lights decorating our house and the presents, and we went caroling around the neighborhood.

"We always had snow in the winter and we went for sleigh rides. We'd go to our neighbors where they had horses, and they would hitch a horse to a sleigh and we would ride all around the community and visit people and drink hot apple cider. A couple of times we traveled to Grandma and Grandpa's house for the Christmas holidays. That was really fun because Grandpa made little toys for all the kids, and Grandma was a baker and she was always making all kinds of Christmas cookies and cakes and pies."

"Oh, I forgot about that!" I said. "We also made Christmas cookies, and we decorated them with frosting, red and green and white. They were these really good sugar cookies – oh, I couldn't eat even one now, they were so sweet! We would make a lot of them and wrap them up in little baskets and take them to elderly people in our neighborhood."

"So, you poisoned old people with sugar?" Kenrick asked. "That's one way to control the population."

"No!" I said. "That was when everybody thought sugar wasn't that bad."

"I don't remember those days," Kenrick said. "I don't think my parents ever ate sugar, so, they didn't let me eat any."

"Christmas cookies and cakes and pies," Big Hawk said. "I remember sugar! It was not like any of these things we have now, all these fruity sweet substitutes. Things made of real sugar tasted really good."

"Taste isn't everything," Kenrick commented.

"You sound like you are full of Prop," Big Hawk told him.

"Hey!" Kenrick said, offended. "I got us here, didn't I?"

"Yes, and we really thank you for it," I said, patting his hand.

"So, we opened our presents on Christmas day," Big Hawk continued, "the ones we were giving to each other, and the ones all our family members sent to us. My grandmas and my aunts would always make these really neat sweaters and scarves, and my uncles and my dad would always build things for us, toys and trains, and things carved from wood, so we had, like, a hundred presents under the tree. Each one of us made something for everyone else in our family, so we were working on our gift list all year. My mom would put up all these gifts in packages, big boxes, and send them to the other families. We would get boxes from all our family members, too, boxes full of presents, and it was really great."

"So, Christmas was all about who got the most presents, and who got the best presents," Kenrick said, scratching his head. "That sounds really great. I wonder why my family didn't participate in it? They were always giving presents, and wanting more stuff, and better and newer stuff."

"It was a Christian holiday," I said. "It wasn't about the presents, that was just a part of it, to show everyone how much we loved them. Christmas was about celebrating the birth of Jesus, and family. It was a family holiday and we all enjoyed celebrating together."

"Yeah, family," Big Hawk said, nodding. "But when we were kids, we placed a big emphasis on the gifts. We just took our families for granted, like they would always be there, but the gifts poured in at Christmas time, and we loved it. We loved our families, too, and even the gifts helped us keep in touch, because after Christmas we contacted everyone who gave us a gift and thanked them. It was a more personal thing than just getting a bunch of stuff."

"I don't really remember the focus at Christmas time being on the gifts," I said. "It was all those things, those traditions, that we did every year together as a family. That's what makes the memories. You know, I haven't even thought about our family Christmas traditions since I came to live at the Complex. Every day at the Complex is just like another, either working or a Mandatory Day Off, without anything special happening, nothing to celebrate."

"Yeah, I do miss celebrating my birthday," Kenrick said, surprising me.

"See?" I said happily. "There's a family tradition for you. Did your mom make you a birthday cake with candles, one for each year, and you got a lot of presents?"

"No, I don't remember ever having a birthday cake," he said thoughtfully. "I do remember my mom would make a special dinner for me, and then after we ate, my mom and dad would give me something to add to my computer, either a new game or a new level or some new kind of a program."

"Comgen," Big Hawk said, letting off a huff. "We ate birthday cake and ice cream, and you got computer programs."

"How do you think Kenny became a Comgen?" I asked. "He had to be immersed in computers and programming every hour of every day, from a very young age."

"Good thing you liked doing that," Big Hawk said. "What if you had been born an Ordinary, who liked to ride bikes or play, instead of sitting at a computer all day?"

"I did not have any choice," Kenrick said matter-of-factly. "I didn't think about doing something else. I just did what my family was doing, and I had to fit in with what they were doing. And I liked it. No, I take that back: I loved it. And I still love it. The things I do, the things I love to do, are now running everything in the world. I can thank my parents for that."

"Speaking of parents," I said, "did you guys know that Hiding Cathy's dad works at the Complex?"

Kenrick and Big Hawk looked at each other. They already knew! By the way they were looking at each other, I could tell they knew something else, too. They answered at the same time.

"Yeah, he does," Kenrick said, nodding, just as Big Hawk was shaking his head and saying, "No, he doesn't."

"Yes, he does," I said. "She told me. He works as a Food Manager and she gets to see him sometimes. Not very often, but she does get to see him. They have to keep it secret." Kenrick and Big Hawk were looking at each other with strange expressions on their faces.

"What?" I asked. "You guys know something. What is it? What? What do you know? How can he work there and not work there?"

They kept looking at each other, as if each one wanted the other one to tell me whatever the big secret was.

"You can tell her," Big Hawk said.

"No, you go ahead," Kenrick said.

"Tell me what?" I asked, looking from one to the other.

"It doesn't matter who tells," Big Hawk said.

"That's right!" I said. "So, someone, tell me, whatever it is! How can her dad work at the Complex and not work there? Why would you both say opposite things at the same time? Either he does or he doesn't, right?"

"You are right," Big Hawk said. Then they were both silent.

"I am right in what way?" I asked. "What do you mean? I was right in the first place, and her dad does work at the Complex? Or I am right in saying that he can't both work there and not work there?"

"Both," Kenrick said. "You are right in both."

"So, her dad *does* work at the Complex?" I asked.

"He did," Kenrick said.

"He did?" I asked. "He did work there, but he doesn't now? So, what is he doing now? Why did he leave his job? Where does a person go when they leave the Complex? I mean, why would anyone leave a good job to go out into a world of uncertainty? Or, did he get fired? Oh, I hope not. Oh, Hiding Cathy doesn't know yet, does she? Oh, no! Poor Hiding Cathy!"

Kenrick and Big Hawk continued looking at each other without saying anything. They both looked down at the table, avoiding my eyes.

"How did you guys know?" I asked, then I realized that was a dumb question. They both had access to the personnel database, and they were sworn to confidentiality, so they knew lots of things they couldn't talk about, or they weren't suppose to talk about, but everyone talked to their friends, didn't they?

"So, where is he now?" I asked.

"He's..." Kenrick said. He looked at his fingers, which were tapping on the table.

I looked from Kenrick to Big Hawk. Why didn't they want to tell me where he was?

"He's in heaven," Big Hawk said. "I mean, if he was a Christian."

"He died?" I asked. "He's dead?"

"That's the only way to get to heaven," Big Hawk said, nodding his head.

"It's nice for you to believe that's where he is," Kenrick said.

"It's not nice for Hiding Cathy!" I shouted.

"She probably already knows by now," Big Hawk said. "I'm sure someone told her."

"She didn't know yesterday," I said.

"They didn't tell her?" Kenrick asked. His mouth dropped open.

"Apparently not," Big Hawk said. "I thought she

already knew by now."

"Why?" I asked. "When did it happen? When did he die?"

"About a year ago," Kenrick said, "according to the reports I read."

"A year ago?" I exclaimed. "Hiding Cathy's dad died a year ago and they haven't told her yet? That is terrible!"

"Well, the connection wasn't official," Kenrick said.

"Connection?" I asked, shaking my head. "What connection are you talking about?"

"The connection between Hiding Cathy and her father," Kenrick explained, which didn't make any sense to me.

"What do you mean?" Then it dawned on me. "Her dad wasn't really her dad?" Now, this was really getting strange.

"No, he really was her dad, but it was a secret," Big Hawk said. "They weren't connected in the database. It didn't specifically say her dad was her dad. There wasn't any official record that said they were related."

"Then how do you know he was really her dad?" I asked, searching their eyes for a clue.

"If you ever saw him, you would have no doubt about it," Big Hawk said. "She looked exactly like him."

"Why didn't I ever know about this?" I asked. "You guys knew – how long have you guys known?"

"I met him a long time ago, a few years ago, and I knew he was her dad," Big Hawk said. "Besides looking just alike, they had similar mannerisms."

"Really?" I asked skeptically. "He liked to scrunch

himself down and hide under things, too, like Hiding Cathy does? What was his name, Hiding Frank?"

"No, not that kind of mannerism," Big Hawk said. "He just had the same kind of silky white hair, and he would toss his head the same way as Hiding Cathy does. And, you know the way she looks at you, like she's almost afraid to look at you?"

"Yeah, you mean, like, looking down, and stuff?" I asked. "Not really making eye contact?"

"Yeah, and just the way she is in your presence," Big Hawk said. "Almost like she is there but not there."

"Yeah, I know what you mean," I said.

"Well, I just found out a couple of weeks ago," Kenrick said. "I never met her dad, but I just happened to be reading some data bank stock that mentioned him, and it mentioned their possible but not proven connection. When I called up his photo, I knew it was her dad."

"Poor Hiding Cathy!" I said again. "She doesn't even know he died! Wait – I think she said she saw him recently, a couple of months ago."

"Well, if she was talking about her real father," Kenrick said, "he died about a year ago."

"And nobody told her about it?" I said, my heart breaking for her. "That's terrible!"

"It was bad enough that they weren't even allowed to talk to each other, or to acknowledge that they were related," Big Hawk said.

"But why not?" I asked. "If they were both needed at the Complex, then why–"

"You know how strict they are against family

connections," Kenrick said. "Any type of sentiment could cause problems. People would want special favors or specific days off, or if someone got sick, they would want the day off or something to see about them or take care of them or visit them in the sick pods."

"Yeah, or they might be worried about each other and not able to work or concentrate," Big Hawk said. "Take away all human feelings for other humans and the Complex will run with all essential efficiency."

"It has been a long time since I have even heard the word 'human,' you know," I said.

"They hope we will forget we are actually human; we are just pegs in a cog," Kenrick said in a monotone voice.

"Peas in a pod," I said, smiling, recalling a phrase my dad used when referring to my mom and my aunt.

"Peas in a pod?" Kenrick asked, shaking his head. "What does that have to do with pegs in a cog?"

"Nothing," I said. "They just sound alike. You know I am always doing puzzles and codes. Sometimes the codes have to do with sound-alikes."

"Yeah, anyway, any type of human connection that they can remove, they have removed," Big Hawk said, "or tried to, at least."

"But what about the ones at the Complex who are married?" I asked. "They are in love. They are trying to start families. They must be sentimental about each other, and starting to have their own traditions."

"Marriage, yes," Big Hawk said, standing up to get something out of a cupboard. "Love, no." He looked at the items before selecting one. He opened another bottle of juice and began to drink it.

"What do you mean, 'love, no'?" I asked. "They have to be in love to get married." I was remembering how much my parents had loved each other. I could see it in their eyes when they looked at each other. My mom had often told me that when I grew up and met the man I would marry, I would know it because I would love him. God would provide me with the man of my dreams. I didn't know yet who that would be, but I was sure I hadn't met him yet. That was fine with me, since I wasn't finished growing up yet. I still had plenty of time for that.

"Do you know any of the married couples at the Complex?" Big Hawk asked.

I tried to think if I did. I knew many of the people at the Complex, but I didn't know any who were married to each other. I knew one or the other, the husband or the wife, but not both. I shook my head. I couldn't think of one single couple that I knew there.

"They – the couples – are put together by arrangement," Big Hawk said. "They are put together for a specific reason, like, if they show signs of both being fertile, they hope they will be able to conceive. Those two people are made into a couple, whether they like each other or not. If two people are able to work very well together, with each one fulfilling specific tasks that work out well when they do them together, they are made into a couple, so they can work on their projects together all the time. There is no room for love at the Complex."

"You can't be serious!" I said. "That is against human nature!"

"There you go again, thinking that we are somehow still human," Kenrick said.

"We are!" I said. "And, when I'm ready, I want to marry the man I love!"

"And, who might that be?" Big Hawk asked teasingly.

"I don't know!" I said. "I probably have not even met him yet!"

"How do you know what love is?" Kenrick asked.

"I remember the love that my parents had for me," I said. "That was real love. I remember how they loved each other, and that was real love between a man and a woman, the way God intended it to be, from the beginning."

"There you go again, assuming God is real and that He made everything, and that He had a purpose for everything," Kenrick said.

"He did, and He does!" I insisted. "When I meet the man God made for me, I will know it. I will love him, and he is the only one I will marry."

"I'm afraid you won't have any choice," Big Hawk said softly.

"Yeah, they are probably trying to set up a match for you already," Kenrick said.

"Why do you say that?" I asked. "I'm too young to think about getting married! What do you know? Who is it? Tell me! Tell me!"

"I don't know of any particular man yet, but your data has been fed into the mix," Kenrick said.

"Into the mix?" I asked, looking at my friends. "What am I, a part of a recipe?"

"It kind of works like that," Big Hawk said, nodding. "You could call it a recipe. That's actually a good name for it."

"I am not some ingredient to be combined with another ingredient to make the best possible dish!" I protested.

"You don't think you are," Big Hawk said, "and I don't think you are, but the State has specific plans for each of us."

"What about you?" I asked. "Do they have a wife selected for you? You are older than I am."

"I'm sure my data has also been fed into the mix," Big Hawk said with a grin. He didn't seem upset. He was looking forward to it!

"You don't care?" I asked. "You are just going to go along with whatever girl they pick for you?"

"We really don't have a choice, do we?" Kenrick asked. He ran his fingers through his glossy black hair.

"What about you?" I asked him. "Are you in the mix, too?"

"Not yet," Kenrick said. "I'm not old enough yet, but I doubt if they will match me with anyone, because they need me to be a Solo-gen when I pass the age of accountability."

"Solo-gen?" I asked. I hadn't heard that term before.

"Yeah, what they call the ones they want to become loners," Big Hawk explained.

"Well, I think it should be your choice," I said. "What if you meet someone you love, someone you want to marry?"

"Even if I do, it won't be allowed," Kenrick said, shrugging his shoulders. He seemed to be satisfied with that.

"Why do you guys both know about this and I don't?" I asked. "Who told you about all this?"

"I hate to break it to you," Big Hawk said, "but men are still in control. Even though they say men and women are equal, they tell us what we need to know–"

"Like, you can't fall in love with anyone?" I interrupted. "Well, you can't control love! They can't control love! If you fall in love with someone, you can't help it. And then they make you marry someone else? No, that is not going to work for me."

"It has to!" Kenrick said. "We have to follow the rules, or we can't stay living at the Complex!"

"We are breaking the rules right now!" I said. "We are not authorized to be on this plane right now!"

"But we are," Kenrick assured me.

"Everything in our records says we have full authorization," Big Hawk said.

"If you can cheat using a computer so we can travel," I said, "then surely there is a way for us to actually love who we marry, and marry who we love."

"You are right," Kenrick said. "I might be able to fix things in a favorable direction for you."

"Just keep my name out of the mix for now," I said.

"I can do that," Kenrick said. "Consider it done."

"Thank you," I said. I knew I could trust him; Kenrick always kept his word. I was still disturbed about the whole situation, though. I knew they had control over us and what we did, but it hadn't sunk in that they had total control over every aspect of our lives. We still had to have some sort of free will.

CHAPTER 6

"I'm going to see if I can fly this thing for awhile," Big Hawk said, standing and stretching. As he went into the cockpit, I looked at Kenrick, who didn't seem at all worried.

"It's all automatic," Kenrick said confidently. "Actually, he can't change a thing. Everything has been pre-programmed. Even if he moves the steering mechanism, he won't be steering the plane. The plane will stay on the pre-designated course. He could take a nap in there and it wouldn't make one bit of difference."

"But there IS a real pilot in there with him," I said.

"Yeah, that, too."

About one minute later, Big Hawk came back into the cabin and sat down with us at the table.

"So, did you fly?" I asked.

"Yes!" he answered excitedly. "Didn't you feel it?"

"Yes, we did," Kenrick said, nodding his head in an exaggerated manner.

"It was really fun," Big Hawk said. "You should try it some time."

"I will," I promised. I didn't really have a desire, but I just said that to keep him from bugging me about it.

"Me, too," Kenrick said.

"Maybe later," I added.

I stood up, browsed through the selection of food and grabbed a package of energy mix from a cabinet. I took a peek out the window and saw we were high above the clouds. I sat down at the table to eat my snack.

"So, I was just wondering," Kenrick said, "what do you guys remember about The Great Devastation itself? I mean, the Day of Devastation?"

"I don't remember it at all," I confessed. I didn't like to be reminded of it. That day was a blank in my life. I couldn't recall one thing that happened that day.

"Besides your wonderful family holidays, what do you remember from your Life Before?" Kenrick asked.

"I can remember bits and pieces," I said, "just flashes of scenes of my mom and my dad and Aunt Moon and Uncle Pierce. They were always smiling and I remember it was always warm in those days." I could remember a few specifics, but my memories of my family were so personal, and, I felt, irrelevant to this conversation, once we began discussing the day of horror, the day my world was torn to shreds and I was left to live out just a little piece of it.

"You were eight when it happened?" Kenrick asked me.

"Yeah, I was eight years old when it happened," I confirmed.

"What about right after?" he asked. "What do you remember?"

I shook my head. "I just remember visiting my mom in a Home a couple of times. I haven't seen her in a long time, but she couldn't even see me or recognize me when I visited her. I don't know what happened. I wanted to go see her again, but it wasn't an option. I was just at the Complex. Before I worked there, I just played a lot of games and read a lot of books." I thought it was strange, they still called them 'books,' even though they were electronic, either on our reading devices or on our Wat-Coms. We didn't have anything like what I remembered as a book from my Life Before. Hmm, there was another flash of a recollection, books made of paper with pictures in full color, turning pages with my hands.

"You said you never left the Complex after you came to live there," Big Hawk said. "So, how did you visit your mom?"

"I don't remember exactly," I said, trying to scan my memory. "I just remember seeing her, but I don't remember going there. I don't remember ever leaving the Complex. I guess I saw her before they brought me to the Complex."

"Probably virtual," Kenrick said. "You were so young, they gave you a virtual experience. That's why she didn't respond. You weren't really there. She might have died a long time ago, and they just saved an image of her to project so you would think you were visiting her."

I felt anger growing as I considered this angle. When I had seen her, she was always in the same position, in a room that was tinted green, and I always entered from the same door and saw her looking the exact same way. They wouldn't let me approach her.

"That's why they didn't let me touch her?" I asked. "Or even get close to her? They told me she could still have some contamination on her."

"That's it," Kenrick said with a sigh. "There was no contamination. They just used that as a way of separating people, keeping the Ordinaries out of the Complex."

"It was all Prop?" I asked. "There was no contamination?"

"You betcha," Big Hawk said, looking at Kenrick. "How old were you, Kenny?"

"I was only six, but I remember everything," he said. "We lived on a farm in the Midwest and my mom and dad discovered that I was really good with computers when I was about two years old. They were trying to get some government assistance, so they told them about me. They gave me game after game after game – I thought I was just playing games – but they were really testing me to see what I could do. When I turned five, they wanted to take me away from my parents and take me to training, and they were going to pay my parents a huge amount of money to use my brain, or, actually, to use me. My parents were kind of unsure, they thought I was too young to leave them, so they were negotiating a deal. The government didn't want me to get away or go astray, but my parents didn't want to lose me.

"One day, before they agreed when to transfer me from my home, we heard about the beginning of the war, and that day there was great confusion everywhere. I was at school, one of the places the government never wanted me to go, but my parents wanted me to start in the first grade. That's where I was, with a room full of kids who were starting to learn their ABCs and the numbers. It was so weird, all these kids around me that were my size, but they seemed like their brains were so dull. They just couldn't communicate with me. They were all like babies and I mostly stayed away from them. So, that day the alarms were sounding and we were taken to our shelter-in-place at the school. We thought it was just a drill, like we had before.

"Then one of the government men came into the shelter-in-place and he told the teachers I had to go with him, that there was a problem with my parents. The teachers didn't want to let me go, but he showed them his credentials, and my teacher asked me if I knew him. He was one of those government guys, and I told my teacher I did know him. She let me go with him. I was really worried about my mom and dad, but when I got in the helicopter with them, they didn't fly me to my home. I was so excited to be in a helicopter, and I asked them why we weren't going home. I could see where we were going and I knew from the virtual map games I played that we were not going toward my house. They told me we were going to meet my parents somewhere, so I sat back and enjoyed the ride. You know, it was amazing how much a real helicopter ride was like a riding in a heli-simulator, only louder. Much louder!

"So, they brought me to the Complex and I never saw my parents again. At first, they told me they were on their way and just hadn't gotten there yet, then later they told me that my parents were killed on the way to meet me. They told me it was a top secret operation and I couldn't talk to anyone about them. They let me have a one week grieving period, then they started training me. They gave me all kinds of games I could play in my pod or at the entertainment area, but really, I was being trained. I caught glimpses of what was happening around the world, with the fires and earthquakes and bombings, but I didn't really understand what it meant, except that lots of people were dying, and my mom and dad were dead.

"I got used to my new life, and, as they coached me, I became thankful that I was still alive and had been rescued in time."

We sat there, our snacks finished, and I thought about what he had told us. I compared my story with his story. We had both been deceived, and we were both being used by the State, after they had lied to us.

"How do we know for sure that our parents are dead?" I asked. "I mean, the population database does not say that my mom is dead, but it says that my dad is dead. How do we know it's right?"

"That whole database is a farce," Big Hawk said. "They had me work on it a couple of years ago, and it is not at all accurate. I looked up some people that I know are dead and it says they are still alive and contaminated. On the other hand, some of the ones I think are still alive, it says they are dead."

"That is a problem with databases," Kenrick said. "When the integrity isn't constantly checked, they can become so corrupt or outdated they are useless. We, at the Complex, rely on all our databases and our technology, and we just assume that because the computer says it's right, it's right. You know, the team who works on the population database has been working on some top-secret project, and they haven't updated the old database in nearly three years, except to add in the new births."

"Are you serious?" I asked. Maybe I had been naïve to assume that all the other people were doing their jobs as they should, because my friends and I always did.

"Yeah, I had to fix some of the coding when we updated the system, and they hadn't done any updating of the data in years," Big Hawk said. "It's not really accurate, either. I saw one area where a bunch of random dates had been entered – some in the future."

"I'm not surprised," Kenrick said. "Would it be reasonable to say they are planning to kill those persons on those dates?"

"Or they'll just let that database die," Big Hawk

said. "They don't really use it anymore."

"But isn't it connected to the implants and the tracking?" I asked.

"That's what they want us to think," Big Hawk said. "They have a new program for tracking Ordinaries they are using now."

"Yeah, I worked on it," Kenrick said. "It's really neat. It places the person right on the map, then we can zoom inside and see just what they are looking at."

"That's why they aren't allowed to wear hats," Big Hawk added.

"Everyone knows that," I said.

"Everyone doesn't know that this system just got up and running in the last month," Kenrick said.

"I thought we had been using it for years," I said.

"That's what they wanted us to think," Big Hawk said, winking at me.

I was a little disappointed. I thought we, the Kidgens and the Comgens, were the free thinkers, the intelligent ones, the ones who were directing things and coming up with new ideas. Now my friends were telling me that I have just been thinking only what I was allowed or conditioned to think. Even though all my needs were supplied and my life was actually a life of ease, I didn't trust the State any more. If they were lying and covering up about one thing, they could be deceiving us on all types of levels. Yes, I could admit that we had been deceptive in our own way, to take this travel without proper authorization, but we were just kids and it was really like a prank, a joke, one that was covered (by the clever manipulation of Kenrick) in every aspect. We weren't hurting anyone or the State. We had finished our duties and we had earned a break.

"Hawk, what about you?" Kenrick asked. "What do you remember about the Day of Devastation?"

Big Hawk looked at the ceiling, as if watching the events of that day.

"I remember it all. I was nine years old, almost ten. I was on vacation with my family at the Grand Canyon and there a few other people around at that time. We were going to hike down and go to the river below and camp down there. We were up on the rim, kind of near the edge, making our way there, when we felt the earth shake. There was no question that it was an earthquake. My dad shouted for us to lie down on the ground and cover our heads. The shaking was really mild, it lasted just a few seconds, and I thought it was over. I got up and walked back, over to where our car was, way back from the edge of the rim on the other side of the road, but my parents and my brother, he was 15, didn't know I was going to the car. I really wanted to get my flashlight I had left there and I was ashamed to tell my parents I had left it because they had asked me if I had everything and I didn't want to let them know I had forgotten something. I went around to the other side of the car and I could see them, my mom and my dad and my brother, and they were lying there, faces down, protecting their heads. I remember thinking, they were so unaware of what I was doing, and since the shaking had stopped, why were they staying there like that?

"Then there was a really big rumble, and in slow motion, I saw a huge chunk of the rim just go down. I mean, where they were, the whole ground just slid into the canyon. It was going so slow, and I could see it, I could see them, right there, and I wondered why they didn't just get up and run back to where I was, where it was safe, but they didn't move, they just let themselves fall down. I tried to call to them, but my voice didn't make any sound. The rumbling was so loud. I couldn't move from where I was. It was like I was watching a life-size movie, a disaster movie, and I couldn't do anything about it. They went over the edge! They just went over, with the ground! I remember seeing my mom's hand reach out, over to where I had been, like she was trying to grab my hand so we could fall together, and then they were gone.

"The car was locked but I knew how to break in. Most of our food was in the backpacks, so I had some with me. I got in the car and I—" Big Hawk stopped for a moment. I tried to imagine how terrible that had been for him, just a boy, to see his family go over the edge of a giant canyon.

"You?" Kenrick prompted.

"I cried," Big Hawk said quietly. "I was afraid to look over the edge or even to get any closer. There were a few more earthquakes or aftershocks, but I just stayed in the car. I ate some food later, I wrapped up in blankets, and I was there for a few days or maybe it could have been a couple of weeks. I got out of the car for a few minutes at a time, then I would get scared so I got back inside the car. One day I heard a helicopter flying over, and I got out of the car and waved my hands. They didn't see me at first, then I got out a big white towel and waved it. They saw me and they dropped down a rescue ladder for me and lifted me up to the helicopter. I told them about my parents and they flew over the area where they had gone down, but they were gone. The whole side of the canyon had collapsed, and they were somewhere under that giant pile of rocks.

"Then they asked me a bunch of questions while

we were in the helicopter and they discovered I was a Kidgen and they brought me to the Complex. That was when they first started calling it the Complex. I used to wonder where they would have taken me if I wasn't a Kidgen."

We sat, silent, for a few minutes. I felt upset. We had never before been able to share our experiences – it was forbidden at the Complex for anyone to discuss the Day of Devastation. I glanced up at Kenrick and I could see that his mind was working. He was planning something; or he was putting into place something he had already planned.

"So, why all the questions about the Day of Devastation?" I asked.

"I may as well tell you now," Kenrick said. "We are going to where it all started."

"Seriously?" Big Hawk said, his eyes growing wide. I didn't know why he was asking. Kenrick was always serious about everything.

"So, you're saying it's not contaminated any more?" I asked. No one had been able to return to the Origin of Devastation because the whole continent had been contaminated.

"It's clean," Kenrick said. "I checked the results of the probes they sent there. It never was contaminated. They just didn't want anyone to go there, or to even think about going there."

"The probe reports–" I began, then I understood what was happening. "The probe reports were fake, like everything else!" I shouted.

"Well, not everything was fake, just some of the important things," Kenrick said. He turned to me and he gave me a strange look, as if he were feeling sorry for me. He lowered his voice and spoke softly to me.

"You know, I almost hate to tell you this, Layla, but you have to know. Now is the time for me to tell you. The codes you decode are just made up for you to decode. We don't really have an enemy out there, just the Prop Resistors, and they don't have any muscle, they don't have any weapons, and most of the time they don't even have enough power to run their appliances."

My mind stopped for a second, a gaping hole of understanding. He wasn't making any sense. "Why do they have me decoding?" I asked. My whole purpose in life was suddenly in question. My work, which they had told me was essential, was completely useless? I was being used to do… nothing?

"Just to keep you ready, to keep your brain sharp," Kenrick said. "Just in case they need your skills someday, they want to be sure you will be ready. They thought it was better for you to not know, but I felt like I had to tell you."

"Thank you," I said, not sure if I should be thankful or not. I stood up and went to the front part of the cabin. I looked out the windows at the blue sky above the plane and at the clouds way down there, below us. I sat near a window and my mind went way back to a time when we, my family and I, went to church and worshipped God. I knew He had created everything and that humans had messed up the world; but God was a forbidden subject at the Complex. My biggest secret from the State was that I believed in God. The State, I was now aware, had multiple secrets they had been keeping from me. How was I going to be able to function when we returned, knowing that we were being deceived in so many ways, and that my job was completely unnecessary? If I told them what I now knew, or even that I suspected it, I would be in big trouble.

I wanted to take a nap, to awaken and not know all that I now knew. My whole life had changed with one sentence. As I tried to relax in the seat, Kenrick came over to me and reminded me to buckle my seat belt while I was resting, so I did. My mind was in turmoil now. I was so angry at them for everything! My whole life was pointless! My work was useless! Even the visits I had made to my mom were not real. How could I go on? Why should I go on? Just to keep up the farce, to pretend I didn't know? Why did they really need me? What were they really using me to do?

I must have dozed, but I didn't feel at all rested. As I looked out the window, it was dark outside, and we were still in the air. Kenrick and Big Hawk were stretched out, sleeping, and I wondered how long the pilot could fly by himself. I went to the wash room and washed my hands and I looked at all the food. I wasn't hungry, but it was comforting to know that the plane was well-stocked, so we could be gone for at least two or three weeks and have plenty of food. I browsed through the selection of clothes and I was not moved to choose anything else to wear. When I returned to the cabin, I notice that Big Hawk wasn't in there sleeping. I could hear him talking to the pilot. I wondered, was his real name Polo? I knew what my real name was. That was one of the few things they hadn't tried to change when I went to live at the Complex.

Suddenly I felt very cold. I grabbed a blanket and cuddled into my seat, again buckling my seat belt. I closed my eyes and I let myself drift away.

CHAPTER 7

"Prepare for landing," the pilot's voice said through the intercom system. "Seats upright and seat belts fastened."

For a moment, I forgot what I had discovered, and, just briefly, I was excited about our travel. Then everything I had recently learned flooded my mind with the bad news and the feelings of gloom and uselessness to go with it. I tried to focus on the fact that we were traveling and we were away from the deceivers at the Complex, even if only for a little while.

"This is going to be great," Kenrick said. "No one has been here since the Day of Devastation. And I mean NO ONE. We are the first."

"Are we there?" I asked, finding my voice.

"We are almost there. We have to land up here, and then we'll take a helicopter to the actual site."

"Who's flying the helicopter?" Big Hawk asked. "Polo?"

"No, I have scheduled another pilot to fly the helicopter," Kenrick said. "He should be waiting for us at the air strip. Polo isn't a heli-pilot."

"So, even the heli-pilot hasn't been there, or here, or wherever we're going?" I asked. It seemed a little odd to fly into a place, even by helicopter, with a pilot who had never been there.

"He will drop us off on a heli-pad and then we will need to walk a few miles," Kenrick said, "so, let's load up our backpacks before we leave the plane. Also, the weather here is a little warmer than it is back home, so let's pick out some appropriate clothing."

I didn't like the fact that Kenrick was calling the Complex 'back home.' It was not my home, and I would never again think if it as such. It was just the place I lived.

As the plane came to a stop, I could see through the window that the sun was just rising, giving a beautiful light over all the landscape. I noticed the helicopter was sitting a short distance from the plane. I changed into a nice, comfortable looking outfit and rolled up another one and stuffed it into my backpack. I put on some shoes that looked like they would be good for walking.

Maybe I could enjoy myself while we were here, and deal with the lies and deception when our escapade was over. Maybe I could find another way to deal with it, by adjusting my attitude or something. Wasn't that the way of our world?

After we washed our hands and grabbed a bite to eat, we loaded our backpacks with food and bottles of water. We climbed down the steps of the plane and stepped onto a sea of gray sand that stretched as far as I could see in every direction. Big Hawk and I followed Kenrick to the helicopter, which seemed to be vacant.

"I wonder where the pilot is?" Kenrick asked aloud. I didn't know why he was asking us; he was the one who had made all the plans and schedules. "It seems weird that the helicopter would be here but not the pilot. I mean, he would have to come here by helicopter. Where could he go? There's nothing around here." He looked around the helicopter.

"And you are asking us?" Big Hawk said, mirroring my thoughts.

"Just talking out loud," Kenrick said. He chuckled. "Or, I mean, I'm just thinking out loud."

We scanned the horizon but we didn't see anyone or anything anywhere. The desert was just bare and flat, as far as we could see. I didn't even see one cactus.

"Let's put our stuff inside the helicopter and I'll try to contact him," Kenrick said. He pulled up his sleeve and I was shocked to see his Wat-Com on his wrist!

"Hey!" I said. "How did you get your Water Closet back? I saw you put it on that cow's leg."

"It's my spare," he said deviously, pressing buttons.

"Spare? Who has a spare Water Closet?" I asked. "Everyone is allowed only one Water Closet."

"Oh, you are surprised he has another one?" Big Hawk said, as if this were a normal occurrence. "Kenny probably has spares of everything. Let me guess. This one has no tracking or monitoring devices?"

"You're close," Kenrick said. "It has them but they are disabled. If an emergency comes up and I need to use it, I can reactivate it. You don't think I would travel without any technology, do you?"

"I just didn't think about it," I said.

"Um, Layla, I think it's time for you to start thinking about things," Big Hawk said gently.

"Yeah, I guess I should," I agreed, although I didn't like the newly discovered information that I now had to ponder.

We approached the helicopter and Kenrick opened it by using his Wat-Com. Just as he was about to sling his backpack into one of the seats, a man popped up inside, out of nowhere, scaring me about half to death.

"You're right on time," he said to Kenrick.

"Wow, we couldn't even see you," Kenrick said. "I

didn't even know you were in there. I was trying to imagine where you could have gone, since there is no place to go around here."

"Likewise, I couldn't even see your plane," the man, who I guessed was the heli-pilot, said, "but I could hear it."

"Yeah, it's the cammy paint," Big Hawk said. "It makes the plane almost invisible. So, are you wearing cammy paint, or how did you hide like that? You weren't there, then, there you were, just like that." He snapped his fingers.

"I was in the pilot's compartment," the heli-pilot said. "For our protection, they put a hidden compartment in every helicopter that can't be seen, and can only be opened from the inside."

"Makes sense," Big Hawk said. I agreed; I just hadn't thought about these types of things until now. Now I was going to start thinking of all kinds of things that weren't taught at the Complex, and I was going to start paying attention to a lot of things that were not my business. After all, in a couple of years I would be an adult, and without the security of my job, I would need to be aware of the world around us. I also needed to learn a useful skill so they would have a reason to keep me at the Complex.

"Are you ready to go?" the pilot asked. "We want to get this flight out of the way before it gets too hot."

"Let's go," Kenrick said.

We climbed into the helicopter and the pilot handed us each a set of ear plugs. I stuck the plugs in my ears (I had left my super hearing device back in my pod, thinking I would not need it while on travel) and I was still shaken when the propellers started. They were much louder than I imagined they would be. I could feel them pounding through my body, shuddering my heart.

As we were flying, not too high off the ground, I searched in vain for another tree. I could see no trees in this part of the world. Kenrick and Big Hawk had a conversation in sign language, but I didn't even look to see what they were saying. I was fascinated by the moving landscape beneath us, and what they were saying couldn't be more important than this excellent view. This was the same way I flew in my dreams, just about this height, just about this speed, and the view was like the view I saw in my flying dreams. The only difference was the sound – my dreams were quiet, and riding in this helicopter was terribly noisy. In a very short time, too short, I thought, since I was really enjoying the ride, we landed on a pad in the middle of nowhere. A huge cloud of dust rose up all around the helicopter, so thick, we couldn't see anything beyond the dust cloud.

The heli-pilot kept the propellers going and signed for us to keep our heads down as we left the helicopter. A door came open beside me. As soon as the three of us jumped out of the helicopter, it rose above us and flew back the way we had come.

I closed my eyes for a minute, to protect them from the flying dust. As soon as it began to settle, I peeked and could see that we were standing on a platform on a little ridge in the desert. I had no idea where in the world we were, I just knew it had taken us a long time to get here. I wondered how Kenrick knew how to get us here, anyway. The location of the Origin of Devastation was not known to anyone, and forbidden. There I was, questioning Kenrick again, knowing full well that he had access to everything and he had information about everything. They thought a 14-year-old wouldn't understand or do anything prohibited with the knowledge he had, but he did what he wanted to do, and he had access to do literally everything that had anything to do with technology, so all doors were open to him.

"This way," Kenrick said, beginning to walk in a direction towards nothing. Big Hawk and I followed him.

We walked a couple of dusty miles before we stopped to drink a little bit of water. Obviously, there was no source of water in this area, so we didn't want to use more than we needed. The morning was cool and clear. I wondered where we would find shelter from the sun when it made its way overhead, but I was sure Kenrick had that planned, along with everything else.

As we were walking, we gradually went down an incline until we were in a great valley. We turned to our left and we continued walking in something like a canyon, where gray, sandy mounds at least a few miles apart rose to our left and right.

"Whoa! That's weird!" Kenrick said. He liked to say things were weird when they didn't fit in his expected realm.

"What?" Big Hawk asked. I thought Kenrick must be referring to our bare surroundings, but he was looking at his spare Wat-Com.

"It stopped working," he said, pushing buttons and trying to reset it. We stood there and watched him for a short time.

"Can't be low on power," Big Hawk said. "There's enough sun here to power the entire Complex for at least a year."

"I read about this but I didn't believe it," Kenrick said. "I thought it was more Prop."

"What are you talking about?" I asked. I was really out of the loop of everything, wasn't I?

"They said in this valley, no instruments can be used," Kenrick explained. "Maybe due to the elements surrounding us, like the hill near the cow barn. They're causing a meltdown."

"A meltdown?" Big Hawk asked. "Really?"

"Not in the terms you would call a meltdown," Kenrick said, "but electronically."

"Yeah, I get it," Big Hawk said, "I just didn't think it was possible. Are any of the features working?"

"No power at all!" Kenrick said, clearly frustrated. "Well, we will have to take care of our business here, where we are going, and then we need to move on from this place. This isn't our final destination." He started walking again, so we did, too.

"It's not?" I asked. "So, what is?"

"Let's finish this business first and I'll tell you where we are going next when we get back to the plane."

I suddenly had to stop.

"Ew! What's that smell?" I asked, holding my nose. A heavy metallic smell was seeping into my senses; I could taste it, even with my nose plugged. It tasted like I had a big metal plate in my mouth.

"It's not that bad," Big Hawk said. "I mean, it isn't exactly pleasant, but it's not that bad."

"It's that bad," I said. I couldn't stand it. It seemed to be seeping into my eyes, burning them. I squinted so my eyes were just slits, to protect them.

"It smells like the electronics storage warehouse," Kenrick said. He actually seemed to be satisfied smelling that awful odor! I couldn't see anything except dust, but I could feel the metallic odor entering my pores and seeping into the insides of my teeth.

As we walked for a few more minutes, the intensity of the odor began to fade, or else I was just getting used to it and it wasn't bothering me as much as it did when we first entered the valley. I was able to remove my hand from my nose, but my eyes were still burning a little. I kept blinking to try to get a little relief in my eyes. We stopped to drink some more water.

"I was just thinking," I said. "It's a good thing Hiding Cathy didn't know where we were going."

"Now you are beginning to think," Kenrick said. "That's one reason I didn't tell you guys anything. Now she can't be forced to tell anyone where we went, if anyone should ask. The other reason was more fun. I wanted to surprise you!"

"Believe me, we are surprised," I said.

"Surprised, indeed!" Big Hawk agreed, showing his big-hearted grin.

"You know, this desert is so different from the desert around the Complex," I noted. "There is no life here! No trees, no bushes, no rabbits..." I didn't really know what other life was in the desert outside the Complex, but those three things I saw yesterday. This was a completely barren land. The sky was a beautiful bright blue, and the sun was rising to a height that might soon begin to bother us.

We walked for a while longer, then Big Hawk

stopped us. "I see something," he said.

"What is it?" I asked. I was straining to see anything but sand, while his hawk eyes were looking at something I couldn't see.

"Up ahead," he said. "It just looks… different."

"Different? What kind of different?" I still couldn't see anything. All the sand looked the same to me.

"That's probably it," Kenrick said. "Keep going."

"Just another sip of water first, please," I said. My lips had become incredibly dry, beginning to crack, and my eyes were burning from lack of moisture.

We drank a little more of our water and then we continued on our trek. We eventually arrived at a place that was somehow different from the miles of sand we had just covered. I could see signs, however faint and vague, that life had existed here at one time. We turned to the right, following an ever so slight path, which led us in another direction, which I instinctively felt was south. We had to follow this path. This path would lead us to our destination. I boldly took the lead. I felt as if I knew where we were; as if this place were familiar to me. I was walking fast, and the guys had to trot to keep up with me.

The desert here wasn't like the rest of the desert. Instead of sand, I saw remnants of a foundation of asphalt beneath us, with the tiniest blades of grass growing up in it, through it, in many places. I could see the slightest tint of green ahead of us. I led my friends on a path that only I could see – because I had seen it before – to a crossroads. When we arrived at the center of the cross, I stopped, overwhelmed, and turned to face north, the direction we had just come.

CHAPTER 8

The memories came flooding back to my mind. I had come home. An odd, dreamlike feeling came over me. I blinked and I could see it clearly. I felt the hair standing up on my arms.

"I remember," I said. I felt as if I were in a trance, being controlled by an outside force, but it was actually my inside force, my own memories returning. Big Hawk and Kenrick stood looking at me. They kind of faded from my vision. I began to speak, just letting the words flow without knowing in advance what I was going to say, as I looked at the thriving community that had once been here.

"We lived here, at Four Quadrants," I began. "This, right here, this very spot, was the center of everything. Right where we are standing was the crossroads of two super highways, each eight lanes wide." I could see it now, just as it had been, full of life, with people buzzing around in every direction.

"Over in that quadrant, the northeast quadrant, was where we lived. That was the residential district, where all the houses and apartments were, going up on that little slope over there. All the residences were a tan color. There were hundreds of them, and they were all built to look just the same. We lived at the back side, way over there. I lived there with my mom, her name was Sun, and my dad, his name was Obiad, Obiad Maloof. My dad was Obiad Maloof." I hadn't thought of their names in such a long time, but now, here, they came to me so naturally. The sound of their names coming out of my mouth was beautiful. My heart felt warmed.

"My Aunt Moon and my Uncle Pierce Steele lived

next door to us. We lived in houses, big houses, made of stone or rock, or something like that, with really thick walls. Even though the weather here would get really hot, the inside of the buildings stayed cool, because of the thickness of the walls. I remember our porch had a wall around it, about three feet tall and it was thick like the walls of the house, and I would climb up on it and sit. My mom and my Aunt Moon did all they could to make our houses look different from the rest of them, but, even with their individual touches, it was hard to tell the houses apart. When we turned on to our block, I would automatically begin to count the houses. The fifth house from the corner was Aunt Moon and Uncle Pierce's house and the sixth house was ours."

"Wait," Big Hawk said, temporarily pulling me out of my long-lost vision. "Your mom was named Sun and your Aunt was named Moon? Did they have a sister named Star and a brother named Comet?"

I shook my head slowly, seeing the past right before my eyes. I ignored his question.

"Shh! Let her tell what happened!" Kenrick said. "Don't interrupt! Nobody else knows this!"

I was transported back in time. I could see the lively city, exactly as it had been when we lived there. "So, we lived over in that quadrant, it was full of houses. Across the freeway in the northwest quadrant was the airport, over there." I pointed in that direction. "The runways were on the back side of the airport, going that way. We passed them as we were walking in here just now. My Uncle Pierce was a pilot, and he flew out from there. We went to the airport a lot. They had some shops where my Aunt Moon loved to shop, and they had really neat stuff from all around the world that we couldn't find anywhere else." I could see the airport, busy with people coming and going.

"Both my Uncle Pierce and my dad worked for the government. They worked at the military base, and it was over in that quadrant, the southeast quadrant." I turned to face that quadrant, which was behind where we were standing, to our right. "The main building was enormous, about eight stories tall," I made its shape with my hands, "and there were all these smaller buildings around it. Everything in that quadrant was kind of a gray color, the color of cement." As I looked in that area, I was picturing how it had been, so dominating and full of life, with flags flying and people going in and out of the buildings all the time; but there was absolutely no remnant of any building or any life in that quadrant now.

"The freeways, where we are standing, were raised up, and the foundations of the buildings in the quadrants were sunk down, on a lower level, if you know what I mean." Now everything was flat, or as flat as it could be with all the sand kind of mounding over it, making it look like the floor of any other canyon in the world.

I turned and pointed to the southwest quadrant. "Over in that quadrant was the Mall, where we went shopping and went to eat and to the movies, and for other activities and entertainment. That was when there were still new movies being made, you know, before the entertainment sides of the United States dropped into the seas and we were left with the movies already made. Anyway, this whole area seemed endless to me when I was little, but I can see where it must have ended, at those hills over there and these hills on this side, with the runways from the airport going down that way to the west, and the east end must have been where that sort of a ridge is, over there." Now it seemed to be about eight miles square, but it could have been larger than that. It was hard to judge the distance when there were no landmarks or buildings as points of measure.

"There were skyways so we could walk over the freeways from one quadrant to another, right over there, and over there, and over there," I said, pointing to where they had been. "My dad and Uncle Pierce walked to work every day, using the east skyway, on this end, and when Uncle Pierce was going to fly, he would walk to the airport, crossing the freeway using the north skyway. When we went to the Mall, we would cross over that skyway to the airport first, then we would cross over to the Mall on the west skyway. I remember my mom and my Aunt Moon were always so happy, and they were so beautiful, both with their blond, curly hair and green eyes. People would often ask them where they got me, since I was so dark, I didn't look as if I belonged with them. But I did. I got my brown hair and brown eyes from my dad."

"Did you go to school?" Big Hawk asked. I glanced at him and saw that he was staring intently at me.

"Shh! Don't interrupt her train of thought!" Kenrick warned. "She's the only living person who was there!"

"No, it's okay," I said, immersed in my memories. I turned so I was facing the southeast quadrant. "The school was at the military base, but I only went part time. We had accelerated learning, and most of the time I was with Mom and Aunt Moon, participating in the activities at the Mall, or at our house or at Aunt Moon's house. My parents taught me most of what I learned at home, and I used the computer and the simulators for learning, too. My mom and Aunt Moon really liked to sing, and they taught me lots of songs and we would sing all the time."

"Well, that was kind of a waste of time, wasn't it?" Kenrick asked.

I shook my head, remembering my happy Life Before. "Back then, we had so much time," I said, "and we enjoyed every minute of it, with each other." I really did enjoy my childhood life much more than my current life at the Complex. Solving puzzles all the time wasn't what it was cracked up to be.

"So, was there lots of traffic going through here?" Big Hawk asked. I could tell he was trying to visualize it. "Where did the cars come from, enough to fill up an eight lane freeway?"

"I don't remember very many cars being here," I said. I was seeing it the way it had been. "There were just a few cars on the freeways. I think the freeways were made for future use, because everyone came and went by plane, and around here, we walked everywhere. Some people rode bikes – our whole family had them, and we went for family rides at times when Dad and Uncle Pierce weren't working – and sometimes we would roller skate around here. It was perfect for skating, the paths were so smooth and wide. Everyone got around from quadrant to quadrant by using our legs, human power. Oh, except for the Dignitaries, they had little solar-powered carts they rode around in, but they didn't go much faster than we did. I skated faster than the carts would go. Yeah, all the walkways and the skyways were really wide; wide enough for the carts and the pedestrians, and the bikes and the skaters.

"The runways went way off that way." I pointed toward the west. "Sometimes we, our whole family, would watch the planes take off and land while we were sitting on our balcony after dinner. Sometimes we would eat at our house, and sometimes we would eat with Aunt Moon and Uncle Pierce, and once in awhile we would all meet at the Mall after Dad and Uncle Pierce got off work and we would eat there and then go to a movie. Sometimes we would all go ice skating. Yes, yes, there was an ice rink inside the mall, on the far side, way over that way. In the auditorium, they had all kinds of activities: sports, performances, dances…"

"Like the Nutcracker ballet?" Big Hawk asked.

"Stop interrupting her train of thought," Kenrick said, jabbing Big Hawk with his elbow.

The train couldn't be interrupted. It was barreling down the track of my memory. I turned to the residential quadrant. "Sometimes when it was really hot, we went swimming. We had eight pools in the residential area, so we could swim and dive and play water volleyball. Sometimes we just went in the kiddie pool to cool off, whatever we felt like doing. My dad and I really loved to swim together. Mom and Aunt Moon just liked to hang around the pool and put their feet in the water. They weren't real swimmers like my dad and I were."

I could picture the pools, with the transplanted greenery growing around them, and not many people swimming. Although the whole place was always abuzz with activity, as I recalled, it was never full. It had been built for a lot more people to come and live there, so we had an abundance of space. Sometimes I would be the only person in the Olympic size pool, with a lifeguard watching me swim. Often we would be the only family skating at the ice rink, or the only family in the movie theater; but we were never the only family eating at the Mall. The restaurants were always busy.

"So, that's it?" Big Hawk asked.

"Oh, sorry, I was just remembering how it was," I

said. The memories were coming faster than I could relay them. My eyes were seeing it as it had been when I lived here, in another life, another time, a happy life, a carefree time when we didn't have to be so cautious as to not say or do the wrong thing. The sky was now as blue as it had been, but everything else was different.

"This place was built to be full of people, but it was not fully occupied yet. I mean, there were lots of people here, but there was still a lot of room for more people. When we went to the military base, it had a lot of people working there. Some of the houses in the residential quadrant were occupied by families. When we went to the airport, a lot of people were there, working and traveling by plane. But now that I think about it, there was a lot of room for more people. Most of the houses were vacant."

"This was going to be the center metropolis of the world," Big Hawk said. "It was said to be the safest place in the world, so the plan was to move as many people as possible to this area, all down that canyon and over that plain. This place was said to be earthquake-proof."

Kenrick and I looked at Big Hawk, curious as to where he had gotten his information about this place. No information existed about this area, except for the fact that it was a secret location where The Great Devastation had started.

"I remember," Big Hawk said, a far-off look in his eyes. "My family was planning to move here, after our travel to the Grand Canyon," he said quietly. "Obviously, we didn't make it."

"This was not the safest place in the world," I said, "and it was definitely NOT earthquake-proof. Look at it!" I shouted, feeling saddened at the thought.

"The bombs–" Big Hawk began, then he stopped himself.

"The bombs," I repeated, not wanting to remember, not wanting those memories to return. I felt the burning of tears behind my eyes. I wanted to stop and relish the wonderful memories that had just awakened in my mind, to go back to the blissful time of my life, the time that had for so long been suppressed in a sealed region of my mind. I wasn't ready to leave that time behind and go to the next phase yet... but that was how it happened. I couldn't stop it then and I couldn't stop it now.

"It started out as a normal day," I began, suddenly remembering it as clearly as if it had been yesterday. My voice became flat, a reluctant narrator.

"It was a really hot time of the year. My dad and Uncle Pierce went to work as usual, at the base, and Uncle Pierce was planning to fly that day. He had just come back from a short flight the day before. I needed a new swimming suit because mine was getting too small for me. My mom and Aunt Moon and I had a plan to walk over to the Mall and then we were going to go back home and go to the pools. We started to go on the skyway to the airport, then we would cross over to the Mall. I remember, it seemed like the perfect day. The sun had not made it too hot yet, and we were walking across toward the airport. We were enjoying a very slight breeze. We were talking about the breeze, since it was so rare to be breezy around here."

I turned and pointed off to our left. "The skyway was right there, that's where we were walking, and my mom and Aunt Moon started laughing about something.

147

I didn't hear what they were saying. I wasn't really paying attention to them, I was just so happy to be with them, and I loved it when they laughed like that, like only sisters could laugh with each other. Their faces were so red, they were beaming at each other, and every time they looked at each other, they would start laughing again. I thought it was great. They were laughing so hard, they had to stop walking. My mom was bending over. She said something about Aunt Moon giving her a side ache, and Aunt Moon said, 'Sun! You are giving ME one!'

"We had to stop walking for a few minutes so they could laugh. I looked over to the airport, hoping to see a plane take off or land, but there was no activity in that quadrant right then. I looked down at the freeway below us and I didn't see any cars either. The day was very quiet, except for the laughter of my mom and Aunt Moon. I felt really good, really happy.

"They pulled themselves together and we walked – actually, I skipped – the rest of the way across the skyway to the Airport Quadrant. Then we walked across the walkway that joined the two skyways. We were over there, and then we crossed over that freeway, the freeway that was right over there, and we got to the Mall. The Mall had a big dome over it, a cement dome, with all the businesses under the dome. Some were indoors and some were outdoors, but they were all under the giant dome.

"It was early in the morning and not many people were at the Mall. Some of the shops weren't even open yet when we got there. My mom and Aunt Moon stopped at a juice bar to get something to drink, but I didn't want anything from there. I just wanted to get my new swimming suit. They were really taking their time, and even though I was really happy to be there with them, I was getting a little impatient. I looking across the Mall at the stores, wondering which one had my swimming suit.

"Then Aunt Moon's personal phone rang. Remember when everyone used to have a personal phone? Before the days of the Wat-Com? She saw it was Uncle Pierce calling, and she answered. Her smile quickly disappeared and she looked really serious all of a sudden. She didn't really say anything to him, just, 'Okay, I love you,' and then she put her phone in her pocket. She grabbed my mom's arm and said, 'We have to go to the airport. Now.' Her voice was kind of shaky. I got scared. She grabbed my arm, too, and she pulled us toward the west skyway, the one we had just crossed. I thought it was strange, they just left their drinks and they didn't even drink them, and we hurried to the airport. We ran across the skyway to the airport. I thought maybe we had to meet a plane that was landing.

"We stopped when we got inside the airport and Aunt Moon was looking around desperately. My mom asked her what was going on, what were we doing at the airport.

"Aunt Moon said, 'We have to get on a plane. Now. Pierce and Obiad will meet us on the plane,' she told us.

"My mom asked her, 'Why? What for?' and I was wondering the same thing. Why were we going on a plane without any of our stuff? Why did we have to go some place in such a hurry? Where were we going?

" 'We have to catch flight 642, it's taking off in just a few minutes,' Aunt Moon said, as she began scanning the flight announcement monitors. Remember when they had those, inside the airports, that had a list of all the flights, when the planes were arriving and departing?"

"Yeah, yeah, we remember," Big Hawk said, bobbing his head. "So, what happened next?"

"I saw on the monitor that flight 642 was about to depart at one of the farthest gates, and I pointed it out. We ran across the airport. We went through the checkpoint and we got to the gate. Uncle Pierce had arranged for our tickets, so we just showed our IDs and got on the plane. A few other people were on it, too, but it wasn't nearly full. Aunt Moon said something to one of the guys in charge, about Uncle Pierce and my dad meeting us, and then we got in our seats. I sat between my mom and my Aunt Moon. Right after we buckled our seat belts, the pilot announced that we couldn't wait for any more passengers and we had to take off right at that very moment. The plane started moving.

"I had no idea that this was an urgent situation, and I told my mom that Uncle Pierce and my dad would catch the next plane. The plane went quickly down the runway and we took off. I heard a really loud noise and everybody started looking out the windows. On both sides of the plane, bombs were exploding all over the place. The plane was shaking, but it was still rising. I was afraid a bomb was going to hit the plane. We were quickly leaving the area, but I saw our house blow up, along with all the other houses near it. I tried to see the military quadrant, but there was so much smoke and fire, I couldn't see anything there. My mom pushed me back in the seat so I couldn't see out the windows any more. I didn't want to see any more. I held on to the hope that my dad and Uncle Pierce had made it to the airport and I just knew that the plane they caught had taken off right after ours.

"I looked to my mom and my Aunt Moon for

encouragement, but they were both on the verge of breaking down in tears. I told them, 'Dad and Uncle Pierce are on the plane right behind us,' and they both started crying. A few minutes later, the pilot made an announcement that our plane was the only plane to escape from there.

"We were flying for a long time. While we were in the air, we heard the news that the war had become global. The place where we had been, Four Quadrants, this place, right here, was where the war had started, and the entire area was completely demolished, with no survivors. We also heard that bombings around the world had triggered earthquakes, and the demolition of the polar ice caps was causing extreme flooding. We were told that entire countries were being covered by water. Our plane eventually landed at the Chicago airport." I tried to swallow the lump that was forming in my throat. Out of the corner of my eye I could see Kenrick nodding his head slowly, as if to confirm my story.

"As soon as we landed, agents separated me from my mom and my Aunt Moon. I kept thinking that there was a mistake on the news announcement, not everyone had been killed, and my dad and Uncle Pierce would show up and come and rescue me. I stayed with a couple, a man and lady, and they told me my mom was really sick and she was in a hospital. They wouldn't let me go visit her or even tell me where she was. They wouldn't tell me anything about my Aunt Moon. They told me there were no survivors of the Four Quadrants, except the 16 people who had been on the plane, and I was lucky to be alive. I didn't feel lucky at all, without my family. My life had completely turned around in just one day.

"They – the people I stayed with – were nice to me, and they gave me all these puzzles to play with. They told me I had a talent for working puzzles, and shortly after that, my life at the Complex began."

I stopped speaking. I was exhausted. All the memories flooding back like that had overwhelmed me. I dropped to the ground, sitting in the dust at the center of the crossroads. Now that I had my memories back, I wondered how I had blocked them out for so long. They were such a huge part of me, of who I was, of who I had been, of who my family was.

The three of us were quiet for quite some time. I sat on the ground without ambition. Had they done me a favor by causing my memories to leave me? Had they improved my life by giving me a job that I had thought was important, necessary to our existence? Or had they ruined me, deep on the inside, by removing from my life the only thing that mattered to me before The Great Devastation: the love and memories of my family?

"I have no doubt that your memories are real," Big Hawk said, "but looking at this place, I can't see it at all. I can't imagine this was a flourishing community. Look at it now. There is no way any kind of life could be sustained here. There's no water, there's no food, there is nothing anyone could use to build a shelter for protection against the sun or the winds that must come through here. There is no way a person could stay alive here for more than a day or two, even if he brought his own food and water."

I couldn't see it his way. I knew how it had been, when we had lived there. My Life Before was still alive in my mind, everywhere I looked. My life had been here. This was where my family had been alive. This was where I had lived. I didn't want to let the images fade; they had been gone from my mind for too long… but the reality was setting in. That was life then, with my family and this was life now, with my friends. The past began to dissolve; I couldn't hold the images any longer.

As I looked around the area, I no longer saw the bustling, rich life that had been there when I was a child. Now I could see what Kenrick and Big Hawk saw: nothing. All that remained was just a huge valley with some small amounts of grass growing where the airport had been, where the giant mall had been, where the military buildings had been, where our home and our lives had been.

CHAPTER 9

Kenrick and Big Hawk took some food out of their backpacks and began to eat. I had no appetite. I stared at the barren landscape and tried to will the scenes of my Life Before, in this area, to return, but now all I could see was the present condition. I could no longer imagine it as it had been. I looked at where the airport had been. I looked at where the mall had been. I looked long and hard at where our house and our neighborhood had been. Everything was gone. Nothing was left.

I turned and looked at where the military base had been. My dad had been killed somewhere between there and the airport. I wondered if he had made it to the skyway, or where exactly he had been when he died. Since Uncle Pierce was a pilot, he must have been informed right before the attack that it was going to happen, and he called Aunt Moon. They had probably wanted him to fly one of the escape planes. Nobody could have known that only one plane would be able to escape before everything – and everyone – was totally destroyed.

As I stared toward the east, Big Hawk looked to see where I was looking. He perked up. I could tell that he saw something, perhaps way in the distance. I stood up quickly, and without any of us saying a word, the three of us began to walk in that direction, on the path that was once one of the great freeways.

I felt hopeful. This was not the same kind of hope that I had of seeing my family in heaven one day, for I held on to that hope for my eternal future, but this was a hope of finding a connection, no matter how small, to my past life at this place. We began walking faster.

I saw something: something not very tall, but something was there, ahead, near the side of the road. I began to run toward it. At first it looked like a cluster of grass that had died because the ground was tinted tan instead of green. As I got closer, I could see hundreds of sticks, standing upright in the ground. No, they weren't just sticks, they were crosses. Hundreds of crosses were stuck in the ground, very close together, little wooden crosses, each just under a foot tall. As we approached them, I could see that they had something written on them, on the cross piece. They each had been labeled with a name. I knew instantly that these crosses had been placed here in memory of those who had died here.

"Crosses," Kenrick said, nodding his head, stating the obvious. "These are crosses."

"Each cross is for a person who lived here and worked here and died here," I told Kenrick and Big Hawk. I didn't know how I knew that, but I was sure of it.

"There must be hundreds of names," Big Hawk said.

"Maybe thousands," Kenrick said.

"Please, help me look!" I said, suddenly frantic. "Help me find my dad's cross!" I had to find it!

We stood there looking at the masses of crosses, and I realized we needed to search in some sort of an organized manner.

"I'll check this group. Kenny, you take that group, and Big Hawk, can you look at those back there? We need to check every one! Please, find the one that says 'Obiad Maloof.' That's my dad's. I need to find it. Help me find my dad's cross!"

I started looking at the names on the crosses in my

section. They didn't seem to be in any order: Kenneth Maroon Bongers, Elfin Josiah Nootch, Hamburg J. Novella, Samuel March Lyons, Jackson St. Jackson, Justin Mac James, Marc Everly Hanson, Luke George Hadley, Dutch Samson Smith, Zach Austin, Freddie Bulsara, Emmett Edward Stout, George Hamilton Joseph, Hammy Sapura, Bon Van Halen, Stinky Malone, Darrell Nashem, Andrew Stemmer, Wilfred Decoto, Victor Ball, Jay Bohannon, Wade Puck Thorson, Wade Carlton, Jerry Barley… none of these names meant anything to me. I wondered if my dad had known any of these men? Some of them might have worked with him.

"Hey, Layla!" Big Hawk called, from his spot, some distance away from me. "Did you say your uncle's name was Pierce Steele?"

"Yes!" I called to him.

"Here's his cross! Do you want it?"

"Where is it?" I asked, going over to where he was standing, weaving through the field of crosses, being careful not to step on any of them.

"It's right here," Big Hawk said, pointing to one of the many crosses stuck in the ground.

"Don't move it," I said. "Just leave it there."

I went over to look at my uncle's cross. Sure enough, his name was hand-written on the cross: Pierce Steele. I thought my dad's cross might be near my uncle's cross, but I didn't see it in that area. I went back to where I had started searching, near the path on the far left side, and the three of us kept looking at the names, but we didn't see one that said 'Obiad Maloof.' Instead of reading all the names, I began to just look at the first letter – it was easy to see when a name didn't begin with an O, so I was able to skim through all the crosses in my area quite quickly. I finished checking one entire section and I stopped to look at Kenrick and Big Hawk.

"I don't see it," I said, shaking my head. They were still scanning the names of the crosses in their sections. I returned to the path, the skimpy path that had once been a great freeway, and I looked again at the hundreds of crosses.

"I don't get it," Big Hawk said, scratching his head.

"What?" I asked.

"If everyone was killed and no one ever came back here, who put these crosses with the names here?"

"Probably some secret military operation," Kenrick said. "Who else would have a list of all these names?"

"Your dad's name isn't in my section," Big Hawk said, gently stepping away from all the crosses in that area.

"It's not anywhere over here, either," Kenrick said, coming back towards me.

As I stared at the crosses near my feet, something colorful caught my eye, something partially buried near the base of one of the crosses, the third one from the path, the one with the name Hamburg J. Novella. I squatted down and reached for the item, to clear off the dirt and see what it was. It was a painted rock that looked like a little egg. As I wiped off the dirt and turned it over, I saw a name was printed on it, in all capital letters: "OBIAD MALOOF."

"I found his name," I said quietly, "but it's not on a cross, it's on an egg. A rock-egg." I curled my fingers around it. It fit so well in the palm of my hand. It felt comforting in my hand. Someone had put my own dad's name on this egg-shaped rock. I looked at the ground again but I didn't see any more rock-eggs.

Kenrick and Big Hawk came over to me so they could look at it. I opened my hand and showed them.

"Why is his name on an egg?" I asked, looking into their eyes, as if they might have an answer. "Why didn't he get a cross, like everyone else?"

"It must be because he was a Christian," Big Hawk said. "An egg represents the new birth."

I nodded. That seemed to make some strange kind of sense to me... but my Uncle Pierce had been a Christian, and others had been Christians who had died here.

I put the egg in the left front pocket of my pants. I somehow felt closer to my dad, now that I had his egg.

"We have to get going," Kenrick said, unusually softly. His voice was normally kind of harsh. "The helicopter will be ready to take us back to the plane in a while, so we have to start walking now."

I wasn't ready to go. I didn't want to leave this place. Time had stopped for me, the one who had a mental clock and could always state the exact time. I had no idea how long we had been there. Had it been minutes, hours, days or weeks? I began to walk slowly down the path in the wrong direction, towards the east, instead of going to the west to join with the path that went north, and out of the Four Quadrant area, back down the valley.

"We have two more places to go," Kenrick said loudly, so I could hear him.

I kept walking, compelled to go away from our intended destination. I didn't care where else we were planning to go, or, rather, where Kenrick had planned for us to go. I couldn't leave this place right at that time.

I was not ready to leave my childhood home, even though it was completely destroyed. This place, this awful, devastated place, was my connection to my past.

"We are going to start walking, and you can catch up with us," Kenrick shouted.

I nodded. Yes, I could catch up with them later, I thought, as I walked toward the ridge ahead of me. The path in this direction was leading out of the valley toward the east, up an incline, and I kept walking. I knew what I had to do, what I should be doing, but I had absolutely no desire to go with them right then. I had to complete this journey first, and close my mental memory book. I would just walk a little ways, just over the ridge, be alone with my grief for a few moments, and then I would turn around and catch up with the guys. I was a good runner, and the day didn't feel as hot as it could have been. I would be able to catch them. They never did walk very fast.

As I continued to walk in the wrong direction, I saw a small hill in the distance ahead of me. I needed to go to that hill, climb to the top, and there I would say my final goodbye. I would let it all go, right up on top of that little hill. Then I could go and catch up with Kenrick and Big Hawk. I first had to go to that hill.

It turned out that the hill was farther than it had seemed at first, but I was determined to get there, to finish my quest. I still had plenty of time to catch up with my friends. I could see my goal, and as soon as I reached it, I would do what I had to do and then I would be ready to leave.

I wasn't really walking very fast myself, I noted. I just needed some time and space to myself. I thought about the rock-egg and the oddness of it all. Why was there only one egg? Or were there more, hidden among the crosses? I hadn't seen the one egg at first, so maybe I had overlooked others? Well, it didn't really matter, because I had the only one that was important to me, my dad's egg. I slipped my fingers in my pocket to feel the reality of the egg. I touched it, traced the shape of it, felt its weight. Then I withdrew my hand, satisfied. The egg was still in my pocket. This egg was a connection to my dad. This egg had been left in that spot, somehow, in the master plan of things, so I could find it. That in itself was a miracle, just for me.

I heard an odd noise in the far distance, a repetitive sound, almost like gunshots, shots from an automatic weapon, the kind some of the radical people had had before The Great Devastation. I stopped walking and looked around at my surroundings. I didn't see anyone or anything, just desert. What was the sound? Where was it coming from? Was it getting nearer to me? If it came toward me, where could I hide? I began walking faster, almost running, toward the only thing that resembled shelter in the whole landscape. The hill was a lot farther than I had first thought it was.

CHAPTER 10

The shooting sound began to retreat into the distance and at that moment I recognized what the sound was. The helicopter was leaving. Kenrick had made a schedule for us, and I didn't follow it. They couldn't wait for me. We had no way of communicating, and I was going in a different direction. However, I was more compelled to keep going in this direction. I felt extraordinarily calm, as if this were my true destiny. I no longer belonged to the Complex; I had no reason to return, unless I needed food, shelter, clothing or companionship. My life and death were ahead of me, here, in this desert, where I had lost my family.

I began to feel the heat of the day and I slowed my pace. I was walking with no real connection to my legs and feet; they were merely carrying me as if I were a stranger to them. I had enough food in the backpack to last a day or two, and enough water to survive for a few days. I wasn't worried. My life had drastically changed one day nine years ago, and now, in one day, it was drastically changing again.

I was approaching the small hill. However, I could see now, it wasn't really a small hill. It looked like it was a type of hut. As I got closer, I saw that in the wrinkle of the landscape, there were actually several small huts in a little cluster. I wondered how old they were? How long had they been there? How had they survived The Great Devastation? Had they been there for thousands of years? What were they made of? I wanted to touch one, to see if they were real. Maybe my imagination was taking over my mind, which wasn't functioning any more; it was just wandering in an automatic mode.

Just as I was nearing the largest and closest hut, an elderly man came out of it. I didn't see a door in the hut. Something like straw parted and he walked right through it. He had long white hair and a long white beard, and he was holding a large stick that looked like a carved staff. He looked like the picture I had in my mind of Moses, from the Bible. He was moving very slowly, yet deliberately. I felt that I must be imagining him; or maybe it was actually Moses and I was in heaven? This didn't fit my picture of heaven, but what did I really know about heaven? I hadn't read any Bible stories since I was 8 years old, and none of the ones I remembered really described heaven.

The man saw me and he stopped. He stepped gingerly over to me – my feet were now rooted to the ground. He looked astonished. He said something to me and I recognized that he was speaking in the Arabic language – but I couldn't understand what he meant. So very long ago, my dad had taught me Arabic, along with several other languages that were no longer used, but I couldn't think of anything to say to this man. I could only remember how to say, 'I love you,' but that didn't seem appropriate to say at this moment.

We stood there for a moment, studying each other's faces. I hadn't been this close to an Outsider since I had been an Outsider – but this was an Outsider that I had no idea existed. He wasn't an Ordinary and he wasn't a Crim or a Chair. He had no implant; he had no scar on his forehead. He had no Wat-Com on his wrist. He was wearing a type of robe. He was a person whose existence was not known by those at the Complex. I wondered what he was thinking about me? He had very kind-looking eyes, as if they revealed a tender heart. He kept looking at me, almost as if he recognized me.

All words escaped me. I couldn't even think of one thing to say in my own language. Instinctively, slowly, my left hand slipped into my pocket, to be sure the egg was still there, and I withdrew the egg. I held my hand out to him so he could see it.

The old man looked at the egg, and two more men came out of one of the small huts. They were talking quietly to each other, and they didn't notice me as they walked into another hut. I then understood that this was a little village, a small society that lived, literally, beneath the radar of the Complex! This was a group of people who were not monitored or controlled in any way by the State!

The old man didn't acknowledge or try to draw the attention of the other men. He just stared at the egg for a long moment. Then he smiled kindly at me. He nodded his head and walked away from me, into a different hut, a hut far to the back of the cluster.

I stood there wondering what had just happened. Had I offended him in some unknown way? What was he doing? Should I go, just keep on walking?

I looked at my dad's name on the egg again, and I slipped it back into my pocket, trying to think of what I should do, when another man came out of the far hut and began to walk toward me. He, like the other men, was very thin, but he had a presence about him that was familiar and comfortable. I knew those eyes. He had my eyes, deep, dark brown, looking at me. He walked over to me and he was looking at me in disbelief. I knew right then I must be dreaming or hallucinating, because this could not be possible. He was the most handsome man in the world, standing right in front of me!

"La-la," he said tenderly, his voice cracking.

"Daddy?" I tried to say. It was him! My dad was right here! This was my dad, my own dad! No one else ever called me La-la! Nobody knew my dad's secret name for me!

We hugged. We hugged. He held me the way only a father can hold his daughter, with strength and assurance and love, something I hadn't felt in so long, something forbidden at the Complex. I felt him crying, and I was crying. Now I knew I had died and gone to heaven, because that was where my dad was! I felt a warmth within my heart that hadn't melted in so many years.

We stayed standing there, holding each other for a long time, it might have been a few days. After a very long time and thousands of tears, my dad put his arm around me and guided me out of the now blistering sun into a small hut. The temperature inside the hut was so much cooler than it was outside, under the sun. My body felt a sweet relief from the heat. My dad showed me to a chair. As my eyes adjusted to the darkness, I saw that no one else was inside the hut, just the two of us. We had had so much time and space between us, I didn't know what to say. I had so many questions, but words didn't seem important now; the true fact was that my dad was alive, and I was with him!

He handed me a cup and poured some water from a pitcher into it. I drank it quickly, as my body was reminding me that I was extremely thirsty, especially after losing those gallons of tears of joy. When I finished the water, I looked at my dad – my own dad! – and I began to cry again. Tears were just flowing, tears that hadn't flowed since I was a child. I didn't feel the need to do anything or accomplish any goal – right now, right here, simply being with my dad was the only thing I wanted to do. We didn't even have to talk. It didn't matter to me. My life was now complete. I was with my dad again. He sat in a chair beside me. He cleared his throat as he looked lovingly into my eyes.

"Have I died and gone to heaven?" he asked me, touching my hand. There was that familiar voice I had forgotten, tender and kind, yet authoritative and direct.

"I was thinking the same thing!" I said, reassured by his touch. He was real!

"But you died in the bombing," he said. "Everyone was killed. Nobody survived."

"No, you died in the bombing!" I said. "Nobody survived!"

"Then we are in heaven, because we are both here," he said.

"I didn't know it was going to be so hot in heaven," I said, "unless we went to–"

"No, we believe in Jesus, so we are assured that we have eternal life in heaven," he insisted. I missed my Christian training. At the Complex, they had done all they could to make me forget what I believed.

"Then we must still be alive," I reasoned.

"Now we are getting somewhere," he said, smiling. Oh, how I had missed that smile! His smile made me smile.

"So," I said, always needing a logical explanation, "if nobody survived, how are you still alive?"

"I could very well be asking you the same question," my dad said.

"I asked you first," I said.

"Do you want some more water?" he asked.

"Yes, please, and I want an answer to go with it."

A kind of shadow crossed his face, and I realized this would be a painful story he would have to tell me. After all, I already knew how it ended – nobody survived... except my dad. How could that be?

He poured another glass of water for me and he again sat near me.

"You have grown up," he began.

I nodded. He didn't really look very much older, just thinner and more tired and much more tan than the last time I had seen him, nine years ago.

"Do you remember the last time I saw you? You were wearing a red dress and you wanted to go swimming, so your mother was going to buy a new swim suit for you."

Again I nodded, not wanting to interrupt him, and not trusting my voice to be able to speak. I hadn't remembered the red dress, but he was correct. I had been wearing one. I had no idea what ever happened to it... but that didn't matter. It was, however, fixed in my dad's memory of the last time he had seen me.

He stopped speaking for a minute and he just looked at me. I knew this memory was as painful for him as it was for me; and the event was as surreal for him as it was for me. I was wondering if I might be imagining this, or perhaps I had fainted in the desert and none of this was real. My dad's voice brought me back to reality. He again cleared his throat.

"Did you get the new swim suit?" he asked.

I shook my head, longing to hear his story. How had he not died on that terrible day? What miracle had saved his life?

"Everyone was killed that day," he said. He shook his head slowly at the memory.

"Daddy, what happened? I thought you died in the bombings."

"I should have died," he said, nodding. "I went to work with Pierce, your Uncle Pierce. We went to the base as usual. Do you know what I did there?"

"Yeah, you did puzzles and stuff," I said. I almost added, "like I do at work," but I wasn't ready to talk about that now, especially now, since I was never going back to that job or the Complex again.

He smiled. "When I first starting working for the military, I was a psychologist, and I did that for a few years while you were young. Then when you were about six, I became a chaplain. It was a similar type of work, having people in all kinds of situations come for counseling, but as a chaplain, I had many more resources available to help my clients. When I was a psychologist and, say, a young wife would come to me after her husband had been killed in the line of duty, all I could offer her were words and human wisdom. The people who were hurting or confused or troubled really just came to me for someone to listen to their problems. Most of the time, they didn't get better.

"I decided to apply for the chaplain's job because then I would have a much greater resource available to me. I could then rely on the wisdom of God, and I could give people encouragement, and, most importantly, hope. I could always give someone hope in God. Every day, as I studied God's Word, I would receive what I needed from Him, to be able to help and give support to everyone who came to me."

I didn't know this about my dad. He had been

helping people every day, and I had thought he was just going to work.

"We received an enormous shipment of Bibles two days before the bombing. One of my duties was to distribute them to anyone who wanted them. That morning, a short time after the last time I saw you and your mother, I went into the warehouse. I was scheduled to work with four other men to get the Bibles organized for distribution. I left Pierce in the office and as I was leaving, I heard him receiving his orders to fly out that morning. I was thinking about how thankful I was that I didn't have to leave you and your mother, and I would be seeing you at home that evening.

"I went to the warehouse, but the other guys hadn't shown up yet. I started checking the stacks of boxes of Bibles by myself. I knew I wouldn't be able to do much until help arrived, because the boxes were huge, and they were stacked floor to ceiling. I was standing in the aisle, between the stacks of boxes, when I heard a bomb explode. It sounded so close. I hit the floor, and I could hear the bombing, near and far. I was lying there, between stacks of boxes of Bibles, and something hit the warehouse. I heard a huge sound and saw a bright flash, like the sun had come and landed right beside me.

"The next thing I knew, it was deathly quiet. I couldn't hear anything. I must have been knocked unconscious. As I opened my eyes, at first I couldn't see, and I wondered if I had been blinded by the flash. Everything was dark. I tried to check if I was injured, and I didn't feel like anything was broken, but I was wedged underneath something and it was pitch black. I could smell all kinds of awful smells, so thick, they were permeating into my skin, into my body, but I couldn't move. I was stuck and I was blind. I didn't know what to do, so I let myself fall asleep. I figured someone would come and help me get out of there." He let out a small sigh.

"I don't know how much time passed, but when I opened my eyes again, I could see. I then guessed that it had been night, it had been too dark to see anything when I was awake earlier. I still didn't hear anyone or anything. I could just smell awful odors, a terrible burning smell. I yelled out, as loud as I could, but nobody answered. Now that it was light, I could see how the boxes had fallen and Bibles were stacked around me. The Word of God literally saved my life!

"So, I wasn't crushed, but I was able to move around a little. After moving little by little for a few hours, I finally got out from under the Bibles. They were all over, not stacked any more, but just all over. As I stood up and looked around, I saw that everything in every direction was destroyed – everything but the Bibles. You know, the Bible says, 'heaven and earth will pass away, but the Word of God will stand forever.' "

"And it did!" I said.

"I called out," he continued, "and I spent the next few days looking all around for any other survivors, but there was no one left alive. All of Four Quadrants was completely destroyed, every building and every person. I knew no planes had been able to take off – Pierce was scheduled to be flying the first flight of the day, and he didn't have time to get to the airport in the few minutes from the time I saw him until the bombing started.

"I searched for his body but I didn't find it. Rubble and destruction covered everything in that quadrant. The fires were burning themselves out. All I could see was black and gray, burned and destroyed. The freeways were crumbled to pieces, ruined. The skyways were gone, crushed. I climbed over, across the blown-up asphalt and concrete to the residential quadrant, hoping it hadn't been bombed, but not a house was left standing. I called and called for you and your mother. I searched and searched. I couldn't find even one thing from our house, but I found a piece of red fabric that I was sure came from the dress you were wearing when I last saw you.

"I kept looking for you for days and weeks. I held on to the hope that you were still alive. After I finished searching the residential quadrant, I went to the Mall quadrant to see if you might have made it over there. I felt that you were still alive! I needed to find you, to rescue you. It was hard to search, because everything was so devastated, and I was finding only partial bodies. I was hoping I would find more survivors, but there were none. There was no one left alive but me." He paused and took a deep breath.

"I was able to find packaged food and bottles of water, enough to keep me alive for awhile. I figured I would die of contamination, but when I was still alive a month later, I knew the bombings had not been toxic. Since the whole valley had been completely annihilated, planes couldn't land there, and I didn't see or hear any helicopters flying over. At night I made shelter back where the Bibles were. You know, the entire area and everyone else was wiped out, but the Bibles survived. Even the boxes the Bibles had been in burned up, but the Word of God survived, and it was what protected me from the bombings. Every day, I read the Bible, which was my only companion. I was greatly comforted by it, even though I was there all alone.

"I didn't know why God had saved my life while He

let everyone else in my life die. I knew it was too far for me to try to walk to the nearest civilization, so I stayed there and looked for food and water every day, early, before it got too hot, and late in the evening, before it was dark, but after it had cooled off a little. The wind storms brought more and more sand to the area, and large sections began to get covered by sand drifts. I did what I could, but I couldn't do much, except to stay alive. I didn't see any animals or bugs or wild beasts. I felt like I was the last person left in the world. I thought it might have been a world war and everyone everywhere had been wiped out, and in that case, I would have been the last person on earth.

"A few times I walked to the ridges around the valley where Four Quadrants had been, to look for any sign of life in any direction. I didn't see anything. I never heard any planes fly over. I was truly alone; yet I was not alone. I knew God was with me, every moment. Whenever I would get to the end of my food supply, I would find more, somewhere else, and it seemed like I found it in places I had already looked. But large portions of the civilization were becoming buried in the sand drifts that were coming through with the wind every evening.

"I lived like this for about four or five months. Then one day I was digging in an area where the Mall had been, looking for more bottles of water. I felt like I hit the jackpot when I uncovered a huge amount of them – I must have found the remains of a warehouse where a huge supply of water had been stored, and it had lots of packaged food in it, too.

"I was pulling it out, because that part of the quadrant was rapidly being covered by sand, and I heard something. I heard sounds that I hadn't heard in such a long time. I stopped what I was doing so I could listen. I thought my mind might be manufacturing the sounds, just because I wanted to hear something besides the blowing wind, but as I stood still, I heard it, and it was real. I could hear voices, and they were getting nearer to me! I couldn't tell from which direction they were coming, so I ran out and stood on the highest mound in the valley, so I could see whoever it was, and they could see me.

"They were traveling nomads. I had no idea there were any in this vicinity, but there they were. I waved at them and ran over to greet them. They spoke Arabic, so I could understand them – but I discovered that I had lost my voice. I could hear them, but I couldn't talk to them. The words would not form and I could no longer speak."

"But you're speaking now," I said.

"Your name was the first word I have been able to say since that terrible day," he said, in a way, sad, and in another way, grateful.

"And now you can't stop speaking," I teased.

"Now I have something to say AND I have someone to say it to," he said, smiling.

I was so happy to be back together with my dad. He hugged me again.

"So, you came to live with them here?" I asked.

"They didn't live here then. They were travelers, but when I showed them all the food and water we could get, they decided to build these huts here, where there is a shelter from the wind. I came with them and we have lived here ever since. We haven't seen anyone else at all, so we thought we were the last men on earth. There are no women here with us now. Some of the men had wives, but they all caught a virus and they died a few years ago."

"How many live here now?" I asked. I was fascinated by this little group of people whose existence was unknown by the State. They lived here all on their own, without any help or assistance, and, it seemed, without technology. They had nobody spying on them or listening to their conversations. They didn't have to do what the State told them to do. They had a freedom, but at what price? They had to fight the elements and they had to get their own food, one way or another, and they didn't have any of the luxuries we had back at the Complex; luxuries, however, that at the moment I couldn't recall. To me, this was the greatest luxury: listening to my dad talk to me.

"We have 18 men left now," he said, "but we have six children. We thought they were the only ones left to repopulate the earth."

"Are you guys going to stay living here?" I asked.

"We hadn't planned to move, but now that you're here…" he began. "Layla, how did you survive? Where have you been all this time?"

"Before I tell you, I just have a question," I said.

"Just one?" my dad asked. "I thought you might have a few hundred questions."

"Well, I do, but let's start with one. If you were the only one left, I mean, I saw all those crosses…"

"I put them there."

"All of them?"

"One for each person who died there."

"You put all those crosses there?"

"I knew every person in Four Quadrants by name."

"You did?"

"Yes, I did. I even put a cross up for you and one for your mother. I thought you died there, too."

"I didn't see those two," I said.

"I put them near where our house had been."

"I didn't look over there," I said.

My dad nodded understandingly.

I reached into my pocket. "I found this."

"You found my egg," he said, smiling, and I saw a tear fall from his cheek.

"I wondered why your name was on a rock-egg and not on a cross."

"My life was starting over. I didn't die there." He smiled at me again.

"I'm so glad," I said. I had a new warmth within me; or, actually, an old feeling from way back was rekindled. My mind was still having a hard time accepting that my dad was actually still alive. This was better than any dream I had ever had. My heart was leaping with joy.

"Your turn," he said.

I nodded, trying to comprehend it all.

"You know, Daddy, it's weird," I began. "When I was little and we were all together, I thought that was the only kind of life I could have. I thought that was the only way I could live, as part of our family, with you and Mom. I couldn't imagine any kind of life other than a life of the three of us, all together. We were my life, all together. Then I was away from you, away from both of you, and I got used to that kind of life, a different kind of life. My feelings were squashed and I got used to that life, all by myself, with my time filled with useless projects and gadgets. And now that I found you again, I can't imagine my life without you in it, every day. I know I am the same person, but I feel like I have lived three different lives. I mean, it's like I was really alive when we were together as a family, and then I just existed for nine years, and now that I am with you again, I am alive again. My heart is alive again."

"It's not weird," he said softly, and I knew he knew exactly what I meant. "What about your mother?" he asked, not meeting my eyes.

"On that day, the last day I saw you, we were going to the Mall," I began, then I had to tell him everything. "Daddy, my mind blocked out that day for nine years. I couldn't remember The Great Devastation, and just today, when I went back to Four Quadrants, I remembered everything."

"The Great Devastation?"

"That's what they call it, the war that started with the bombings at Four Quadrants on the Day of Devastation."

"They? Who are they?"

"Okay, I'll tell you what happened. Okay, where was I? Oh, yes, we were going to the Mall, Mom and Aunt Moon and I, and they started laughing about something, really hard, remember how they used to do that?"

"I do remember," he said, nodding.

"Anyway, right when we got to the Mall, Uncle Pierce called Aunt Moon on her personal phone and told her we had to go and meet him and you at the airport, and we were going to fly somewhere. We had to go right away, right at that minute, and we couldn't get anything to bring with us. We didn't even have time to buy a swimming suit." I realized how shallow that sounded, but at the time, I had no idea how serious the situation was.

"Pierce knew," my dad said, sitting back in his chair. "So, he made it to the plane?"

"No, he didn't make it," I said quietly. "We went to the plane and the pilot said they couldn't wait for any more passengers and the plane took off right away. Just as we were taking off, we saw explosions all around. Ours was the only plane to escape. Nobody else got out alive... except you, but we didn't know that."

"He was probably looking for me when he was killed," my dad said.

"It's not your fault," I said. "You didn't even know what was going on."

"Why?" my dad asked, shaking his head. "Why did they have the war?"

"I don't know, but why did they ever have any war?"

"Good question. I never could answer it, except to say that war is in the heart of man," he said.

"You have been reading the Bible a lot." I smiled at my dad.

"I read it every day," he said. "So, you got away. So... where is your mother now?"

"I'm not sure. When we got away from here, we finally landed in Chicago, and we were separated. I don't know what happened to Aunt Moon, but they let me see Mom a few times, but she was like she was in a coma or something, and she couldn't see me. They took me away from her, to live at the Complex."

"The Complex?"

"Well, they call the war 'The Great Devastation' because nearly all of the civilizations of the world were destroyed. During the war, the extreme bombings triggered earthquakes and since the bombs destroyed the polar ice caps, there was also severe flooding. Both the east and west coast of the United States were flooded. That country is now just a state. Only part of what was the mid-west is left, and that is where the Complex is. The only technology in the world is centered at the Complex. That's where all the leaders live."

"And that's where you live?" he asked, raising his eyebrows.

"I did, but I don't live there any more."

"Okay, finish the story. I guess it's not a story, but, anyway, finish telling me about your life since we were together."

"Well, this is what they told me, but now I think it was all a lie. I don't know, I just know that I don't trust them and I don't ever want to go back there. They said I was a Kidgen, a kid genius–"

"I knew that."

"ANYWAY, they took me to the Complex, along with other Kidgens and the Comgens, computer geniuses, and they made the Complex into a high-tech fortress where the Dignitaries live. The Complex is a huge building, bigger than the Mall, where people live and work and eat and play. Only certain people are allowed to leave. I mean, we could go outside the building and skate or swim or run around the path, but only certain people with special permission can go outside the wall. There are cameras and listening devices everywhere. We had to wear these special devices called Wat-Coms on our wrists so they could track where we went, and they could listen to our conversations, and they could communicate with us through them. I left mine on the leg of a cow before we came here."

My dad laughed out loud, that bellowing laugh I hadn't heard for so many years. "A cow?"

It was rather funny.

"Really, I strapped it to a cow's leg." I started laughing, too.

"You left your high tech device on a cow's leg." He laughed again. Oh, how I had missed that laugh! "How did you get back here?"

"Wait, I'm not there yet," I said. "Let me get to that part."

"Okay, no hurry. We have nothing if we don't have time," he said, still laughing.

"A truer statement was never made." I still felt like laughing.

"So?" he asked.

"Anyway, they had me doing this job of solving puzzles and decoding codes. Some other kids and I worked together, and I have three really good friends at the Complex. Well, they aren't all at the Complex right now, but anyway, we worked together, but on different projects. I thought I was doing a great job for the State. I thought I was performing an essential function, and I just found out–"

"Only what we do for Christ will last," he said, turning his palms upward.

"Exactly! No, I know that, but, what?"

"What did you just find out?" He smiled at me.

"I just found out that my work was totally useless. I thought I was decoding real codes and solving real problems, helping with the security of the State–"

"But they just had you playing games, practicing? Not really solving real problems?"

"Yes!" I looked at him closely. "How did you know?"

"I worked for them, remember? Even though it was a long time ago, but the mind set hasn't changed."

"Yes. You are right. The mind set hasn't changed!"

"So, how did you escape and come halfway around the world?"

"Is that where we are? Halfway around the world?"

"If you came from Chicago," he said.

"One of my friends, Kenrick, is a Comgen and a Kidgen. He is so smart with computers, he can do anything. He set up and programmed all of the systems we have at the Complex, and also, outside the Complex. They have all these cameras and monitors set up so they can watch all the Ordinaries and the Crims, the criminals, who, by the way, have these computer chips implanted in their foreheads so they can't go anywhere without being monitored." My dad's forehead was beautifully bare: no scar, no implant.

"Who has time to monitor every person?" he asked. "Are half the people monitoring the other half?"

"They don't actually monitor every person, but they let them know any person can be monitored at any time. They have the technology and the ability, so they can find out if anyone is trying to cause any trouble or anything."

"You don't have a scar on your forehead," he observed.

"No, the Insiders, the ones who live in the Complex, don't have implants. We have our Wat-Coms instead. But I no longer have mine, so they will never find me again. They might find the cow."

"I see," he said. I wondered if he could possibly see the horror of it all. But then, he had lived the past nine years in the desert, thinking his family had all died, so, yes, he could see it.

"Kenrick arranged for four of us to take a travel. He set up everything in the computers, so we had permission to leave, and when he told us to go, we went. But one of our friends, Hiding Cathy, this really nice girl who is really small, and she is, by the way, a spy, well, we almost got caught at the airport and she jumped in and saved us, but she sacrificed her travel. Kenrick and our other friend, Big Hawk, and I got on a plane and a pilot flew us over here. He landed kind of far away, and then we took a helicopter to get closer to Four Quadrants, then we walked the rest of the way in to the area. No one else has ever come here since The Great Devastation. They – the State – said the whole area was contaminated, so no one would risk their lives to go there. But Kenrick found out it was all a cover up, and he wanted to bring us somewhere no one had been, to Four Quadrants, to see the Origin of Devastation.

"When we got there, all the memories I had blocked out for all that time came back to me."

My dad nodded thoughtfully.

"You know," I said, "I wonder if Kenrick knew I had been there on that day? Did he bring us here to see if I could remember? Or maybe he had no idea?

Anyway, we came here and I remembered everything that happened that day. It was like I was reliving it, I could see it so clearly."

"Yes," my dad said softly.

"We were walking around and looking around, and I was telling them all about how life was at Four Quadrants, and what happened that day. Then we saw the crosses, and it dawned on me why they were there. We started looking for your cross, but we couldn't find it. Then I found the rock, the egg, with your name on it, and I felt like I had to start walking in this direction, to get away, to reconcile my feelings, to somehow find what I had lost."

"You did," he said, nodding.

"I did! I lost you and I found you. I walked for a while and then, now, here I am."

"Where are your friends now?"

"They had to go back to meet the helicopter, and I was going to join them, but I had to come this way first. Then I heard the helicopter leaving while I was on my way here. They had to take off without me. So, I am here for good, I guess."

"It is good you are here," my dad said, smiling.

Everlasting Publishing
PO Box 1061
Yakima, Washington 98907
USA

Novels by Dana Pride

The Red Cloak
Nightmares of Murder
No One Like You
Existing
All These Things
Kissing a Dead Man

Other Books by Dana Pride

We Choose Our Memories:
  Sayings of the Old Folks
We Choose Our Memories:
  Sayings of the Young Folks

Poetry Books by Joseph Fram

Joseph's Journey, Volume 1
Joseph's Journey, Volume 2
Joseph's Journey, Volume 3
Joseph's Journey, Volume 4
Joseph's Journey, Volume 5
Joseph's Journey, Volume 6
Joseph's Journey, Volume 7

Other titles available:

Nathan is Nathan, by Jahla
Nathan Art: Autistic-Artistic by Nathan

Now also available to download as e-books!

http://everlastingpublishing.org

http://danabooks.8k.com

www.ingramcontent.com/pod-product-compliance
Lightning Source LLC
Chambersburg PA
CBHW071234130626
46556CB00003B/1005